BLOOD
ON THE
WALL

BLOOD
ON THE
WALL

Jim Eldridge

ROBERT HALE · LONDON

ISBN 978-0-7198-0855-5

Robert Hale Limited
Clerkenwell House
Clerkenwell Green
London EC1R 0HT

www.halebooks.com

2 4 6 8 10 9 7 5 3 1

Typeset in 11/16½ New Century Schoolbook
Printed in Great Britain by the MPG Books Group,
Bodmin and King's Lynn

For Lynne, my constant inspiration

ONE

The body hung like a sack of potatoes; the ankles lashed together with strong electrical wire, tied round and round the thick branch of the tree. The head hung downwards, the whole body swaying slightly in the light breeze. The sounds of night echoed across the ancient stones, muffled slightly by the trees.

Here, this is the place where there was fire and sword, where they died in their thousands. Yet who remembers me?

The gloved hand grasped the knife, held the handle firmly, watched the light of the moon shining through the trees glint as it caught the blade. A good blade, a wide blade, strong, sharp as any razor, honed so fine it could cut through skin, muscle and bone with one blow. But there was no need for force now, the first sacrifice had been made; now there was just the second act.

The other gloved hand took hold of the hair, hanging slack down from the head, and gently turned the body. The sightless eyes gazed blankly, a trickle of blood running down the face from one nostril and into the open eyes, the blood already drying and crusting.

The knife was placed against the neck, almost loving in its caress. A movement, an incision, and suddenly the body jerked as if it had come back to life again as the blood gushed out in a waterfall of black.

It was over almost too quickly, but tonight, here in the open, it would be foolish to take chances. Now there was just the head, that precious object, giver of life, home of the brain, seat of the soul.

The knife cut across the front of the throat, biting deeply, severing the windpipe and the food canal in one cut. A second cut, even deeper, and the head dropped back, hanging now by the spinal cords at the neck. Even in the semi-darkness, the large wound gaped like a second open mouth.

A third cut across the back of the neck with practised ease, slicing through bone, through marrow, and the head dropped, suspended now by just a muscle at each side of the neck.

The muscles, with no brain to guide them, no nervous system to tell them to tighten, stretched.

The blade flash once, then twice, and with a dull and heavy thud the head came away and hit the ground.

TWO

Andreas Georgiou sat on the bench at the end of Bowness on Solway and looked out over the Solway Firth. It was low tide with a few hours still on the ebb before it turned back to flood, and the haaf-netters were on their way out, their huge fishing frames balanced on their shoulders, the nets dangling beneath, their canvas bags for their catch slung over their backs.

Haaf-netting had been a way of life here on the Solway for a thousand years, ever since the Vikings had first introduced it. That's what his friends in the village told him, so it must be true. The fishermen stood up to their chests in the channels of the Solway, holding the long wooden beam that held the net, waiting for the salmon and trout to come past them on their way out to the Irish Sea.

There were just a handful of haaf-netters now; mainly men in their forties and fifties. Very few youngsters were taking it up. It was hard, standing to chest-height for up to four hours in water that swirled and raced as the currents pushed along the channels. It could be dangerous: the sands and mud-flats shifted constantly. Where yesterday the mud was firm under a boot, today it could be quicksand, dragging a man down. There were things hidden in the mud of the Solway: the carcasses of cattle and horses that had been sucked down, tractors that had disappeared long ago. And there were said to be the bodies of children beneath the mud, sucked down by the moving sands while they played, unsuspecting that the tide had turned.

The Solway could be beautiful and cruel at the same time. The tide here was one of the fastest in the British Isles, rolling in at thirty miles an hour. If you were caught on the sands in the middle of the Solway as the tide rushed in, you had no chance. A man wearing heavy rubber waders couldn't run across mud and through sinking quicksands at a speed fast enough to escape. That's why the haaf-netters fished on the ebb. Men who fished on a flood tide stayed close by the shore.

Georgiou's mobile phone rang, the sudden noise cutting through the peace and quiet and he cursed himself for leaving it switched on. Force of habit.

He checked the number displayed on the screen. It wasn't one he recognised.

'Georgiou.'

'Ted Armstrong.'

Georgiou was surprised. Ted Armstrong. The chairman of the Police Authority.

'Where are you?' came Armstrong's voice. There was something wrong with it, a slur in the words, too many catches of breath. It sounded as if Armstrong was forcing out the words through clenched teeth, forcing himself to talk.

'Why?' asked Georgiou.

'I'm outside your house,' said Armstrong. 'I need to see you. Now.'

Georgiou felt annoyed. He had never found it easy to take orders from people who he knew had less brains than he did. Now he had no need to even pretend to be polite to those on the Police Authority who were trying to kick him out of the job he loved. Up till twenty-four hours ago he'd been Detective Inspector Georgiou. Now he was suspended for 'alleged brutality', and the word was he wouldn't be getting back. Early retirement. At thirty-four years of age. The bastards.

'I'm busy,' he said.

There was another sound, a sniffling and a cough, and Georgiou realised with a shock that Armstrong was crying.

'Please . . .' sobbed Armstrong. 'I have to see you. I'm begging you. It's my daughter.'

Kids, thought Georgiou bitterly. They get you coming and going.

'I'm on my way,' he said.

He cut the connection on his mobile and began to walk up the hill back into the village.

Georgiou found Ted Armstrong sitting in his car outside his front door. Armstrong's car was an expensive-looking Audi, fitting for a rich and successful businessman who liked to show off his wealth. Another reason why Georgiou couldn't stand the man. But it was hard to keep up his feelings of dislike when Armstrong was so obviously in distress. Armstrong got out of his car as he saw Georgiou approach. He had stopped crying, but his eyes were red from weeping and his face was deathly white.

'Tamara's been killed,' he said. 'The bastard cut . . .' And then Armstrong stopped and screwed his eyes up, took deep breaths.

'Let's go inside,' said Georgiou.

Once indoors, Georgiou fixed Armstrong a whisky. He looked like he needed something stronger than tea or coffee.

Georgiou waited for Armstrong to recover himself. Armstrong sat perched on the edge of the settee in Georgiou's living room, sipping at the whisky.

'Tamara was murdered last night,' he said at last, doing his best to keep his voice steady. 'Her body was found early this morning, hanging from a tree in Stanwix. Her head was missing.'

Another one, thought Georgiou. There had been a similar murder about a month before, just across the border at Haltwhistle in Northumberland. The headless body of a woman found hanging inside a shed near the railway line

'Why have you come to see me?' he asked.

'I want you to find the maniac who did it.'

Georgiou shook his head.

'That's a job for the police. You suspended me, remember.'

'That wasn't my fault!' blurted out Armstrong. 'I voted to keep you in. It was the rest of them. That councillor who's always going on about civil liberties. Maitland. You did yourself no good when you beat up that kid . . .'

'He was not a kid, he was seventeen, and I was restraining him while he resisted arrest. He had a screwdriver, for God's sake!'

'He said he was an electrician, it was a tool of his trade.'

'An electrician who hadn't worked for six months. What sort of trade is that?'

'That's beside the point . . .'

'No, it is exactly the point. You hire and fire the police, you get the police you choose. You chose not to have me. But now it suits you . . .'

'Andreas, this is my daughter! She was murdered last night by some lunatic . . . some maniac! He cut her head off!'

'And what can I do? I've been suspended.'

'Please. I know I can get your suspension overturned. I've already been on to some of the others on the Police Authority, seeing what I can do. The truth is that most of the so-called detectives at HQ couldn't find their own arses!'

'There are plenty of good coppers there, if you give them a chance to do their job. DS Tennyson, DS Seward—'

'I need you for this!' cut in Armstrong. 'You can find him.'

Armstrong looked at Georgiou, his eyes bloodshot red with tears and pain.

'Please,' he begged. 'Please. She was all I had.'

THREE

After Armstrong had gone, Georgiou switched on his computer and checked the internet news. His first instinct had been to phone the station, talk to Mac Tennyson or Debby Seward to find out the facts, but he was still suspended. They'd talk to him, but they wouldn't be able to give him the information he needed, not without putting themselves in trouble. Armstrong was in no fit state at the moment to give him all the details, so instead he'd have to find out the same way any other member of the public would.

Reading the news reports, he was able to piece the picture together.

Tamara Armstrong was eighteen years old. She'd finished at sixth form and was intending to go to university to study law when the new academic year started. She'd been out with some friends the previous night in Carlisle, and had told her friends she was going to walk home.

At six o'clock in the morning her body had been found hanging upside-down from a tree in a small park near Stanwix by a man walking his dog. Her head was missing. The reports simply said that police were investigating.

It was just like the other murder. Both times the heads had been taken, and neither had been found since. Why? He needed to get a look at the file on Tamara's murder, compare the details with the one in Northumberland, but there was no chance of that while he was suspended. One thing was sure, he wasn't going to be kicked out of the force without a fight. If Georgiou was anything, it was stubborn. It came from being an outsider: half-Greek, half-English.

His mother, Mary, had been a Londoner. His father had been Othonas Georgiou, a Greek-Cypriot waiter she'd met and fallen in love with and married. A year later, soon after young Andreas had been born in north London, Othonas Georgiou had disappeared with the attractive lady cashier from the restaurant where they both worked. The young Andreas's mother had been shocked, but after the initial shock, she decided that Othonas would come back to her.

Of course, he never did. Where he and his cashier had gone, no one seemed to know. The most likely place seemed to be Cyprus, or perhaps Greece. But there was no word from his father, or his father's family, ever again. It was as if the shame had put up a barrier between his father's family in Nicosia and his mother in England, and for some reason his father's family blamed Georgiou's mother for the marital break-up. All that Georgiou had of his father was a photograph taken with his mother soon after they had been married.

When he had been growing up, having a Greek name and an English accent hadn't been a problem for young Andreas. In the part of London where he came from, Camden Town, there were plenty of children of different nationalities.

The problems had surfaced when he left school and decided to make a career in the police. The interview board had looked at his name and raised questions: was he a British national? Did he have a British passport? Did he have any political allegiances with Greek organisations? Did he have a negative attitude towards Turkey and Turkish people?

At first Georgiou had thought these attitudes were amusing. After all, he was English, born in England, spoke English, and had never been to either Cyprus or Greece in his life. But then, when these doubts about him persisted, even after he had joined the force, he became angry. He complained about the way he was viewed, as some kind of Middle-Eastern subversive just because of his name. Someone suggested, possibly with the best of intentions, that he might not suffer these problems if he anglicized his name, became Andrew George, for example.

Georgiou had rejected the suggestion out of hand. Why should he change his name? It wouldn't make any difference to the person he was. 'No,' his adviser had said, 'but it will make a difference to how people think of you before they meet you.'

It was true. If he had an appointment with anyone, as soon as they saw his name, Andreas Georgiou, they expected someone like Zorba the bloody Greek, moustached and dancing and smashing china plates and drinking ouzo. Instead, they were greeted by this very self-contained English detective inspector, quiet, thoughtful, slightly reserved. The antithesis of Zorba.

Georgiou was twenty-two years old when his mother

died, still waiting for Othonas to return. After the funeral, Georgiou had gone on holiday to Cyprus and Greece, curious to get a glimpse of his father's heritage. Cyprus had depressed him, with the naked tribal hatred between the Greeks in the south and the Turks in the north. In fact he hadn't even been allowed into the north of the island, despite having a British passport, purely because of his Greek name.

Greece itself hadn't been much better. The native Greeks seemed suspicious of him because he had a Greek name but his manner and speech were so obviously English. He didn't fit in Greece. And, because of his name, he didn't really fit into the Englishness of the police force. But he had persisted in his ambition, worked hard, proved himself. Progressed from uniform to detective, and worked his way up to inspector, although he'd had to leave London and come to Cumbria to get the promotion. He guessed even in Cumbria, inspector would be as high as he would go. To the people at the very top, to those who made the appointments, he would still be 'the Greek'. The outsider.

To hell with them all. He liked being an outsider. It gave him an edge with everyone. No one could fit him into a comfortable pigeonhole. Except one: husband of Susannah, the most comfortable pigeonhole he'd ever known. Ten years they'd had together, and now she was gone. Dead. And once more, he was 'the Greek'. On his own.

He picked up the photograph of her on the mantelpiece and looked down at her, smiling up at him. If only she was still smiling up at him. But all good things die, that's what they say. Why? So many questions, and only stupid answers.

He thought about the reason he'd been suspended, and anger rose up in him again.

There had been a series of attacks on elderly women on the Raffles estate in Carlisle: straightforward muggings, their bags snatched and knocked to the ground if they resisted. A whisper had given one of Georgiou's snouts the name of the mugger: seventeen-year-old Ian Parks, who lived with his parents and sisters on the estate. The Parks family had a reputation as trouble: their front garden was littered with rubbish, bits of old cars, old scrap metal. Any attempts by the council to get them to clean it up had met with a torrent of verbal abuse, and in one case threats of violence. But the council worker who'd been threatened had refused to press charges. Too scared, thought Georgiou.

Ian Parks had started to train as an electrician when he was sixteen, but had dropped out and now joined the rest of the family in doing little except slouching in front of the TV during the day and annoying the neighbours. It was rumoured he had a drugs problem. This information came as no surprise to Georgiou – Parks's parents were virtually both alcoholics. If the addiction gene wasn't genetic, it was certainly an influence on Ian Parks's growing up. Georgiou found it hard to understand why on earth Councillor Maitland was such a strong supporter of the Parks family.

All the muggings had taken place at around half past six, when it was still broad daylight. So Georgiou had set up a watch on the Parkses' house from an unmarked car from 6.15 p.m., and assigned two of his DCs, Richard Little and Kirsty Taggart, to keep the house under observation from a discreet distance.

For the first three days nothing out of the ordinary happened. Ian Parks and his sisters had come out of the house and gone to the local shop, and then come back again. Little and Taggart had taken turns to follow him.

On the fourth day, Little phoned, claiming he had flu. Georgiou suspected it was just a bad cold: Little was a prissy soul and a bit of a hypochondriac. He had been going to put another of his detectives on the case, but in the end decided he'd do the shift with Taggart himself. He had little else to do with his life except work, ever since Susannah had died.

At 6.40 that evening Ian Parks came out of his house and headed in the direction of the local shopping precinct. Georgiou followed on foot, with Taggart following in the car. As Parks neared the precinct, he suddenly made for an old lady who was coming back from the shops. He grabbed the handbag she was carrying and pulled at it, throwing the old lady off her balance. The woman hung on to the strap of her bag, but Parks tugged harder at it and pulled her over. Georgiou was already breaking into a run.

Parks heard the sound of running footsteps, turned and saw Georgiou heading for him, and immediately let go of the woman's bag and ran for it. Taggart appeared in the car, the driver's window rolled down, and Georgiou pointed at the fallen woman and shouted 'Look after her!' as he ran off in pursuit of Parks.

Parks may have been younger than Georgiou, but his lifestyle meant he wasn't as fit, and Georgiou was soon catching up with him. Parks suddenly stopped and whirled round, pulling a screwdriver out of his pocket as he did so, and holding it menacingly towards Georgiou.

'Back off!' yelled Parks. He looked panicky.

Georgiou took a step forward, and Parks thrust at him with the screwdriver. Georgiou swayed aside from it and caught Parks's wrist, twisted it, and then punched Parks hard in the face with his other fist.

Parks staggered, and then Georgiou twisted his arm, forcing him down onto his knees, his face close to the pavement. Blood dripped from Parks's nose and he dropped the screwdriver.

'I am arresting you for assault with intent to commit a theft,' said Georgiou. 'You have the right to remain silent, but anything you do say will be taken down and may be used in evidence.'

With that Georgiou jerked Parks back to his feet, and then handcuffed him.

'I didn't do nuffin'!' protested Parks.

'In that case you've got nothing to worry about,' grunted Georgiou. He used his handkerchief to pick the screwdriver up from the ground, put it in his pocket, and then hauled Parks in the direction of the car.

Within minutes word of the arrest had spread around the estate, and within an hour Parks's father had put in an appearance at the police station, demanding to see his son. Georgiou had dealt with Mr Parks himself, and had found him to be a loud-mouthed, blustering bully who had tried to shout Georgiou into releasing Ian Parks. Georgiou refused, advising Mr Parks that Ian Parks was under arrest.

Two hours later Mr Parks returned, this time accompanied by Councillor John Maitland, who demanded to know what was going on. Georgiou told Maitland that a case was under investigation and a report would be issued in due time.

An hour later, as Georgiou was signing off and about to go home, a solicitor appeared who said he had been ordered to act for Ian Parks and demanded that he see his client. Georgiou assumed that the solicitor had been brought in by Maitland.

The solicitor spent time with Ian Parks, and then left.

Parks was held overnight in the cells, and when he appeared in the magistrates court the next day, the solicitor turned the whole event round: his client, he claimed, had been offering to help Mrs Izmir, the old lady, with her shopping, when a man had appeared who seemed very threatening. Because there had been a lot of muggings on the estate recently, Ian Parks assumed the man was a mugger who was intending to rob him, and so Parks ran away. The man chased after him. At no time did the man identify himself as a police officer. The man caught him and then assaulted him very badly. The solicitor said he would be producing a statement from the old lady concerned to confirm that the young lad had offered to help her with her shopping, and that she had been shocked when the man had run towards them. The solicitor suggested that the whole case be dropped, but the Crown Prosecution Service, acting on the advice of the police, said they intended to proceed with the case against Ian Parks. The solicitor asked for bail for his client while the defence was prepared. Bail was granted and Parks was released.

Later, Mrs Izmir had been brought to the station by Mr Parks to make a statement confirming that Ian had offered to carry her shopping on the occasion in question, and that she had not been mugged. According to the desk sergeant who met them when they came in, and DC Debby Seward who had taken Mrs Izmir's statement, the old lady looked terrified. There was no doubt at all in Georgiou's mind that she had been threatened by Parks.

However, Georgiou had what he believed was an ace up his sleeve: the statement that Mrs Izmir had made to Kirsty Taggart immediately after the assault. It was one of the things that Georgiou insisted on with his team: 'Get a statement immediately before they have time to forget things or make things up. Get it while things are still fresh in their mind.'

So Kirsty Taggart had got a signed statement from Mrs Izmir stating that Ian Parks had tried to pull her handbag from her, and in doing it had pulled her over so that she fell to the ground. Parks had then run off when a man ran towards them.

It should have been enough to settle the case, but it wasn't. The Parks family and Councillor Maitland had taken the story to the local press, accusing Georgiou of police brutality on an innocent boy, and of putting pressure on the witness to make a false statement. The fact that Maitland was on the Police Authority gave him more clout, and he used it. Before Georgiou knew what was happening, Maitland had tabled a motion for the Police Authority asking that Georgiou be suspended until a full investigation of the events had been carried out.

Georgiou and his team thought the motion would be easily dismissed. After all, he had Mrs Izmir's statement.

But he had no witnesses to back him up. Kirsty Taggart had stayed with Mrs Izmir to help her recover and take her statement. However, there were witnesses who had seen Georgiou grab Parks by the arm, punch him, and force him to the ground. None of them mentioned anything about seeing Parks holding a screwdriver. Parks claimed it had fallen from his pocket when Georgiou forced him to the ground. The reason he had a screwdriver in his pocket, he said, was because he had been fixing an electrical socket at home and had put the screwdriver there afterwards, a story backed up by his parents.

The result was that the Police Authority had voted by seven to five to suspend Georgiou from duty while an investigation was carried out. And rumour said that Maitland was already hard at work trying to drum up evidence of other examples of Georgiou being heavy-handed with suspects. And if not Georgiou, then any officer on the force. If Maitland could prove there was a culture of police brutality in the Cumbrian police, then Georgiou would be the scapegoat. And Georgiou knew there would be examples unearthed: drunks arrested with a slight excess of zeal on a Friday night; drug dealers and muggers banged against a wall maybe a little too hard. But one thing was for sure: Georgiou wasn't going to go down without a fight. He'd show the Parks family and Councillor bloody Maitland what they were up against.

The phone ringing brought him out of his reverie.

'Georgiou,' he said.

It was Armstrong.

'The suspension's lifted. You're back on the job.'

FOUR

Georgiou drove from Bowness towards Carlisle along the coast road that ran alongside the Solway Firth. Colleagues in Carlisle asked him why on earth he lived out in such a remote place. 'It's the end of the earth,' they said. 'There's a pub and that's all. Nothing is out there. No take-aways, no chippy. You ought to be in Carlisle where things are happening.'

You're wrong, he thought. Bowness is where things are happening: real things. The magnificent sight of the thousands and thousands of geese that flew along the Solway at the start of every October, come from the Arctic to spend the winter on the Solway marshes. The herons. The wild swans. Oystercatchers, curlews.

Five years ago, in London, he'd been barely able to tell a pigeon from a crow. Now he could identify a bird from a distance by the way it moved in the air, from its silhouette as it waded on the mudflats.

The sun was hot through the car windows, and he opened them wide. Summer had started. He drove across the expanse of marsh, past the signs that said 'Road liable to tidal flooding. When water reaches this point it is two feet deep'. At·least twice a year the road between Carlisle and Bowness flooded, the sea pouring across the marsh and over the road like a causeway. His colleagues in Carlisle said they wouldn't be able to cope with it. It was another aspect of living out on the peninsula that Georgiou loved, the fact that the forces of nature were always present: flood and storm striking at will. You learned to live with it, and respect it.

It had been Susannah who had first suggested they move here. They were both worried about what was happening in London: murder rates rising, violent crime, robbery. They agreed it was no place to raise children, and they both wanted children. They had decided on two: one boy and one girl. Or two boys or two girls. It didn't matter. They just felt that they didn't want their child to be an only child. Georgiou and Susannah had both been only children, and both felt they'd missed out growing up. A child needed a brother or sister as a friend, as a companion, or as someone else in the family to annoy.

Susannah had suggested Cumbria. She said it was far away from everywhere, especially dangerous cities. Georgiou checked the crime statistics: according to them it appeared to be one of the safest places in Britain.

Prices of property in the Lake District and south Cumbria came as a shock to both of them. The influx of southerners buying up properties as second homes or 'investment opportunities' pushed prices sky-high, so they looked further afield.

They found a house they could afford in Bowness on

Solway, a small village of some 250 people on the Solway coast, fourteen miles west of Carlisle. The house was one in a small terrace: three decent-sized bedrooms, a living room and a kitchen, plus a tiny room that would serve as a study for Georgiou. There was also a garden at the back that looked out across the Solway Firth to Eastriggs in Scotland.

During the time they searched for their new home, Georgiou had applied for a transfer to the Cumbria force, and luckily for him, it coincided with the Home Office looking at Cumbria and deciding that the Cumbrian police force did not have enough officers from 'minority or ethnic communities'.

Georgiou had built up a good reputation as an efficient detective during his time with the Met, but he was sure it was the 'ethnic' tag that had landed him the job with the Carlisle force. He may have sounded English, but his type of spoken English was London, which was virtually a foreign language to most Cumbrians. And there was his name: Andreas Georgiou. Greek. Ethnic. A minority nationality, especially in Cumbria. Georgiou got the transfer, and the promotion to detective inspector, and he and Susannah moved to their new home.

Susannah got herself a job in a solicitor's office in Carlisle. It was a stopgap while they waited for their first baby to come along. A year after they arrived in Bowness, Susannah gave birth. Or, rather, almost gave birth. The baby was stillborn. It was a boy. They'd given him a name: Paul.

Then came the bad news. Susannah was ill. Very ill. Cancer. They didn't know where it had come from, what had caused it . . . but then they had to admit that they didn't know a great deal about the causes of cancer. All they did know was that it had got into her lymph system and was now attacking her liver, as well as most of her other organs.

Four months later, Susannah was dead.

In the three months after her death, Georgiou worked all the hours he could, taking all the spare shifts there were, just to keep him from being alone in the house. He considered selling up and moving. But where to? In his heart he felt that Susannah was still here, still with him at Bowness. He couldn't leave because to leave would be leaving her.

And so he stayed.

As his car bumped over the cattle grid that signified the end of the marsh and the entry into Burgh by Sands, and the road away from the coast to Carlisle, he knew that Susannah was with him. That she always would be.

The drive from Burgh into the outskirts of Carlisle was mercifully free of traffic. Now and then a tractor came out of one of the farms and trundled along at twenty-five miles an hour before turning into a field, forcing Georgiou to stay behind it at low speed because the road twisted and turned with many blind bends; too dangerous to try overtaking. And once he had to slow down for a pack of cyclists bent low over their handlebars. On the back of the rear bicycle a battered placard fluttered which read: 'We're cycling the wall.'

At this time of year, summer, the road between Bowness and Carlisle was packed with people walking Hadrian's Wall. They came in all shapes and sizes, and all sorts of costumes. Once he had even seen a group of Roman soldiers in full kit, complete with heavy metal helmets and swords, and the legion's eagle on a pole, marching steadfastly across the marsh. Most of those who did the wall on foot came off at Burgh by Sands and continued their marathon along the specially made Hadrian's Wall Trail, a gravel footpath some of the way, and tracks across fields elsewhere. But the cyclists stayed on the road. And not all of them were on modern bikes. Georgiou had seen five huge penny-farthings wobbling along precariously. All for charity, of course. But at what cost? Blisters on the feet. Sore shoulders from the rucksacks. And if anyone had fallen off one of those penny-farthing bicycles, it would have meant a few weeks in hospital. Still, they were all having fun in their own way. Georgiou just wished they wouldn't do it where he lived.

Georgiou's quiet drive ended when he turned off Burgh Road into Carlisle's Newtown Road. A long line of traffic was backed up along the road. He cursed as he remembered that roadworks were happening in Newtown Road this week. Water pipes being renewed or something. If it wasn't that, it was the electricity cables. Or any of a dozen reasons why the road was being dug up yet again. The heat of the sun in the car, warm in the countryside, was suddenly stifling here in the city, even on the outskirts.

He calmed himself down and turned on the radio, tuning in to BBC Radio Cumbria just as the traffic report came on. The cheerful-voiced girl confirmed that there were indeed roadworks in Newtown and Port Roads and delays should be expected. There were also delays on the M6 due to roadworks, on the A595 due to an accident, and on the trains due to a signal failure.

'The whole country's grinding into gridlock,' grunted Georgiou to himself sourly. But at least it wasn't as bad here in north Cumbria as it was in, say, London and the south-east. There, some commuters spent six hours a day stuck in traffic or on overcrowded trains getting to and from work. A nightmare, by any standards.

Finally, after what seemed like an eternity, but was actually only fifteen minutes, Georgiou made it past the Cumberland Infirmary, and out of Port Road at the McVities' roundabout and onto Bridge Street and Castle Way, the dual carriageway.

Georgiou managed to find a parking space outside the large circular tower known as the Courts, the temporary home for the Carlisle police force following the severe floods, at the bottom of English Street. With their official HQ out of action the police had been moved into this old building as a 'temporary measure', while the flood damage in their old HQ was being repaired. More than three years on and they were still in the ancient building. Among the officers they were running a book on how long it would be before they could move back. Georgiou had bet it would take two years. He'd lost his bet already.

As Georgiou walked into police HQ, the first person he met was the duty desk sergeant, Andy Graham.

'Morning, Inspector,' said Graham, beaming. 'Heard you were coming back. Great news!'

'Thanks.' Georgiou nodded

'Double whammy for you, in a manner of speaking, eh?' continued Graham, still smiling.

Georgiou looked at him, puzzled.

'The football,' said Graham. 'Last night.'

Inwardly, Georgiou groaned. He'd watched the match on TV. England versus Greece. It had been a dreadful game, ending in a 0-0 draw. Not worth watching.

'Nil-nil,' laughed Graham. 'I mean, against England, that's the equivalent of a win for you Greeks.'

Georgiou wanted to say: I'm not Greek, I'm English. But it would be a waste of breath. Georgiou reflected that other people had always suffered like this. Someone with an Irish surname like Murphy or O'Connell was always going to be called Paddy, even if they'd had no Irish antecedents for generations. Somewhere back there in the mists of time was Irishness, so convention said that person would be fond of Guinness and have a touch of the Blarney about them.

'I've got one thing to say to you, Sergeant,' said Georgiou with a sly smile. 'Euro 2004.'

Sergeant Graham shifted uncomfortably. The sergeant was a deeply patriotic football fan, and wasn't fond of being reminded of key defeats inflicted on his beloved England football team, nor of being reminded that rank outsiders Greece had won the 2004 Euro tournament.

'Boss!'

The sound of the cheerful voice made Georgiou turn. His DS, Mac Tennyson, was heading towards him along the high-ceilinged corridor, a broad beam on his face and one hand outstretched in greeting. In his other hand was a half-eaten Mars Bar. Tennyson liked sweets and beer, and it showed in the stomach pushing at his lower shirt buttons.

Georgiou took Tennyson's hand and shook it firmly.

'That's got to be the shortest suspension on record, boss!' laughed Tennyson happily.

'No bribes changed hands, I can assure you,' said Georgiou.

Tennyson gestured towards the stairs.

'Superintendent Stokes left a message that he wants to see you before you start,' he said.

'To congratulate me, I suppose,' commented Georgiou wryly.

Georgiou had little time for Stokes. As far as Georgiou was concerned, the superintendent was a career politician posing as a policeman. Shaking all the right hands, preferably with a Masonic flourish. Smiling at all the right people. Appearing at all the right gala evenings and celebratory dinners. Playing golf with the right contacts. And, most of all, desperate not to make any waves that might upset The Authorities. Catch lots of speeding motorists to keep the statistics of 'crimes solved' sweet, and make sure the paperwork was in order.

'Where are the rest of the team?' asked Georgiou.

'Out checking evidence and taking witness statements,' replied Tennyson.

'Anything from the path lab on the body?' asked Georgiou.

Tennyson shook his head. 'I was just going over there to get the report,' he said.

'Is that why you're munching before you go?' asked Georgiou, grinning. 'Building up your strength?'

'Lunch,' explained Tennyson, taking a bite of the Mars Bar.

'I'll come with you,' said Georgiou.

'What about the superintendent?'

'OK, I'll see him first,' groaned Georgiou. 'While I'm with our lord and master, get messages to the rest of the team. I want them all back here for a debriefing session at twelve. Not just on Tamara Armstrong, but whatever we've got on the killing at Haltwhistle.'

Tennyson nodded. 'I had the info sent over from the Northumbria force yesterday, as soon as I saw the connection.'

'Good,' said Georgiou. 'OK, I'll go and see Stokes. See you in a minute.'

Tennyson nodded and headed off to contact the rest of the team, still munching, while Georgiou mounted the stairs to Stokes's sanctuary, a wood-panelled office whose walls were adorned with framed photos of the superintendent with various local politicians and businessmen, and a shelf laden with trophies.

Stokes called 'Come in!' to Georgiou's knock, and waved an arm at a chair, inviting Georgiou to sit down, but the expression on the superintendent's face wasn't one of welcome. The lack of air-conditioning in the ancient building showed in the fact that the superintendent had his windows open, and a large fan blowing lukewarm air across his desk. Neither seemed to make the superintendent's office any cooler.

'This is a bad business,' Stokes said as Georgiou sat down. 'Ted Armstrong must have pulled in a lot of favours.'

'I'm grateful to him,' said Georgiou.

'You won't be once questions start being asked,' said Stokes.

'With respect, sir, I did nothing wrong when I arrested that youth. I did nothing wrong to get my suspension lifted. It was the decision of the Police Authority.'

'Not all of them,' said Stokes. 'Councillor Maitland isn't at all happy. He's already been on the phone to me suggesting some sort of collusion between you and Armstrong.'

'What sort of collusion?'

'He didn't say. He just wondered why a police officer who was suspended by the Police Authority suddenly gets his job back without an enquiry into the reasons for the suspension. He thinks there's been some sort of cover-up.'

Georgiou wanted to say 'Councillor Maitland ought to be asked questions about his relationship with the Parks family', but instead he just said, 'Councillor Maitland is welcome to ask for an enquiry. That's his right as a member of the Police Authority.'

'But he won't because Ted Armstrong got you back, and at the moment there's a feeling of sympathy among most of the members of the Police Authority because Ted's daughter has just been murdered,' said Stokes.

Georgiou nodded.

'The thing is, Inspector, you'd better make sure you're clean as a whistle in everything you do from now on. Everything by the book, because certain people will be watching you.'

'Councillor Maitland.'

'Not just him. The family of the boy you . . . you . . .'

'Restrained,' said Georgiou politely. 'Ian Parks. The one they claim I beat up.'

Stokes nodded.

'They've already been on to the press,' he said unhappily. 'I had the *News and Star* on to me first thing this morning, asking for my comments about your reinstatement in view of the allegations against you.'

'What did you tell them?' asked Georgiou.

'I told them it was a decision by the Police Authority. If they wanted a comment they should talk to them.'

You gutless piece of work, thought Georgiou sourly. Why didn't you say 'I'm delighted that Inspector Georgiou has returned to work'? Show some support for me. Because that's not your style. Don't rock the boat. Sit on the fence.

'I suppose Councillor Maitland told the Parks family,' mused Georgiou.

Stokes nodded.

'That's my guess,' he said. 'Anyway, you're back. But be warned, Maitland will be watching you. Remember what I just said, you do everything by the book. You take a suspect into custody – any suspect – I want there to be witnesses who see you do it. Reliable witnesses.'

'Yes, sir,' said Georgiou.

'Armstrong's given you a chance. You can repay him by finding this lunatic who killed his daughter. But you do it—'

'By the book,' finished Georgiou.

'Right,' said Stokes. Then he added: 'And do it quickly. People are getting rattled. Two murders in a month, both with the heads taken. If the press are right and this is the same killer as the one in Northumberland then it's a nightmare. We've got a serial killer on our hands. We've never had this sort of thing here before, ever. It's got to be stopped.'

'Yes, sir,' said Georgiou, getting up from the chair.

As he walked down the stairs, he reflected how much he despised Stokes. Stokes didn't want a quick result on this because he was worried about who might be next, he wanted a quick result because he was worried that the statistics reflected badly on him. Two murders. OK, one was in Northumberland, but only just over the border. People would be asking questions about how competent the police force was, and those questions might look at how competent Superintendent Stokes was. Georgiou had the answer to that already: bloody useless.

Tennyson was waiting for Georgiou at the bottom of the stairs.

'I got hold of the rest of the team, guv,' he said. 'They'll all be in the briefing room at twelve.'

'Good,' said Georgiou. 'Let's go.'

Georgiou and Tennyson were just about to leave the building, when a voice behind them called out: 'Inspector Georgiou!'

Georgiou turned. It was one of the civilian support workers, Madeleine Wills.

'Yes, Mrs Wills?' he asked.

'There's a phone call for you,' she said.

'Who is it?'

'Jenny McAndrew from the *News and Star*. This is the third time she's been on the phone for you.'

'Tell her I'm out,' said Georgiou, and turned to walk out of the building.

'But I told her I was going to get you,' protested Mrs Wills unhappily.

'Tell her you missed me,' said Georgiou.

'It might be better if you get it over and done with, boss,' murmured Tennyson. 'She'll only try and get hold of you later. And she might do it at a *really* inconvenient time.'

Georgiou thought it over. Tennyson was right. The last thing he needed was a reporter dogging his footsteps.

'OK,' he said. He pointed to the nearest phone. 'Put it through to here.'

Jenny McAndrew had a boisterous but intense voice on the phone.

'Inspector,' she boomed. 'You're a hard man to get hold of.'

'But I'm here now,' said Georgiou. 'What can I do for you?'

'I understand that you've been reinstated after being suspended,' said McAndrew. 'Is that so?'

'Yes,' said Georgiou, 'I understand that, too.'

'And why do you think that is?' asked McAndrew.

'I assume because the Police Authority have decided I had no case to answer in the charges that were brought against me.'

'By Ian Parks?'

'I don't know who made the charges against me, Ms McAndrew. If you tell me it was Ian Parks, then I thank you for that information.'

'Oh, don't be coy, Inspector,' said McAndrews. 'You're not going to pretend you don't know why you were suspended.'

Georgiou let a second lapse to contain his rising feeling of anger. He didn't like the tone this woman was using, but he wasn't going to give her the satisfaction of losing his temper with her.

'Is there a point to this conversation, Ms McAndrew?' he

asked. 'Only I am very busy. There was a murder yesterday and we're doing our best to investigate it.'

'The second one using the same method,' said McAndrew. 'But that's not why I'm calling. I'm asking if you have any comment to the statement that Mrs Parks, Ian's mother, has given to the press today.'

'As I haven't heard Mrs Parks's statement, I'm afraid I can't comment on it, ' replied Georgiou.

'I'll read it to you,' said McAndrew; and before Georgiou could tell her not to bother, she had started: '"This is an absolute disgrace. This man beats up my poor innocent son and gets let off, just because he's a copper. He's done this before. He's a violent man and he ought to be in jail. There is a cover-up going on here. I am demanding a public enquiry. I want justice done."' There was the rustle of a piece of paper being put to one side, then McAndrew asked: 'What do you have to say to that?'

A lot, thought Georgiou. Like if your son is so innocent, Mrs Parks, how come he has a reputation for beating up and robbing old ladies on your estate? The only reason Ian Parks had never been charged was because his victims were too frightened to give evidence against him. Instead Georgiou said: 'At this moment I have no comment to make.'

'But you would support a public enquiry in order to clear your name?' persisted McAndrew.

'As I said, at this moment I have no comment to make. Thank you for your call, Ms McAndrew.'

With that Georgiou hung up.

He turned to see Tennyson smiling.

'Well done, boss,' his DS said, with a wink. 'I bet she was

hoping to make you lose your rag. You Greeks are supposed to have a fiery temper, after all.'

I'm not Greek, Georgiou groaned inwardly. I'm English.

He headed for the door one more time and said, 'Come on, Mac. Let's go find out what they've learnt from the body.'

FIVE

The path lab had a smell to it like no other place that Georgiou knew. It was like a surgical ward, a butcher's shop and a funeral parlour, all mixed up in the smell of formaldehyde. The headless remains of Tamara Armstrong lay on a metal tray, the skin marble white. The pathologist, Dr Mary Kirtle, indicated the gaping open wound that was the neck.

'A large, very sharp knife was used,' she said. 'Broad bladed. Not serrated. He even cut through the spinal cord and the trachea with it, straight cuts. No sawing.'

'You think he knew what he was doing?' asked Georgiou. 'Someone in the trade? A butcher?'

'Maybe,' said Kirtle. 'But then, you can get instructions from the internet for everything these days. How to carry out your own brain surgery.'

'Would he need to be strong?' asked Georgiou.

Tennyson remained near the door. It wasn't that he was upset by the sight of dead bodies, it was the smell of the place he hated.

'Strong enough in the wrists,' said Kirtle. 'Like I say, no

sawing, so the blade went straight through when pressed. And he was cutting horizontally, not vertically. He cut the head off while the body was hanging upside-down. That takes strength and skill. No chance of being able to use downward pressure to cut through the bone. Mind, it was a very, very sharp blade. Look at the surface of the cut.'

Georgiou examined the cut on the neck: like a joint of meat.

'Whoever it was keeps their knives in very good condition,' said Kirtle. 'Fastidious. We're talking someone who looks after things very carefully.'

'What about the rest?' asked Georgiou, indicating the body laid out on the table. Even in death, you could see that the body was young. Thin, long legs, long arms, hardly a blemish on her, except for the bruised ruts in the skin of her wrists and her ankles.

Kirtle gestured towards the marks on the dead girl's wrists.

'She struggled after she was tied up. See how the skin has been worn and broken by the electric flex. Unfortunately for her, whoever tied her up did too good a job. Again, someone who knew what they were doing, and were very careful to do it right.'

Kirtle moved to the body's hands and lifted one for Georgiou to see. Rigor mortis was already losing its rigid grip on the body.

'However, there's no sign of anything that could be thought of as a struggle before she was tied up. I checked the fingernails and skin of the hands.'

'So she knew him,' said Georgiou.

'It seems likely,' said Kirtle, nodding. 'She wasn't drunk, that's for sure. Not only the level of alcohol in her blood—'

'—but the fact she was walking home,' finished Georgiou.

'Exactly,' said Kirtle.

'Any sign of sexual interference?' Georgiou asked.

Kirtle shook her head.

'No,' she said. 'Not even any attempt.'

'Maybe he's impotent,' mused Georgiou.

'That doesn't stop many of them trying,' said Kirtle. 'They can't get it up but they can still ejaculate. Nothing. No sign of semen.'

'Fingerprints?'

It was a long shot, but Georgiou knew of cases where a fingerprint had been left on a victim's eyeball.

Again, Kirtle shook her head.

'Forensics will be your best answer on this, but to me it looks like whoever did it was wearing gloves.'

Georgiou studied the headless body silently for a minute, then said: 'Nothing that says which sex the murderer was?'

'Sorry,' replied Kirtle, shrugging. 'No semen. No saliva. No body fluids. No marks on the body, except the wire and the knife blade. I'll tell you one thing, though . . .'

Georgiou waited.

Kirtle indicated the open wound that was the neck.

'It's quite likely that whoever did it, they got splashed with blood. She was bled like an animal at a slaughterhouse before her head was cut off. That's a lot of blood to pour out. It would have splashed when it hit the ground. Possibly spurted over the killer. Either they were wearing some kind of protective clothing, which they got rid of later, or they went home with their clothes covered in blood. Someone must have seen them.'

'OK.' Georgiou nodded. 'Thanks.'

'Maybe forensics will have something more,' said Kirtle.

'Maybe,' said Georgiou. 'But if he – or she – is as careful as you say, we can't count on it.'

SIX

As Georgiou and Tennyson walked into the briefing room at police HQ for the twelve o'clock meeting, Georgiou was embarrassed when the four detectives waiting for him broke into a round of applause.

'Well done, chief!' called out Iain Conway, a fierce, tall-looking Scot in his late twenties. If Tennyson lived on a diet that seemed to consist of sweets and beer, Conway was a health-food nut. Plus high proteins and vitamins. With his muscular neck and shoulders, Georgiou sometimes wondered if Conway added steroids to his 'muscle-building' diet. 'You showed the bastards!' finished Conway victoriously.

Georgiou smiled self-consciously.

'Thanks for that,' he said. 'But just because I appear to be off the hook for the moment, don't let it fool you. If we don't clear up the murder of Armstrong's daughter, then we're all at risk of being kicked out for the slightest infringement, real or imagined.'

'While the villains get away with a slap on the wrist,' said Conway, scowling.

As the murmur of voices agreed with this sentiment,

Georgiou again raised his hand to calm the team down.

'We'll deal with the politicians later,' he said. 'Let's look at the case first. Because I've been away for a few days, I'm going to let Mac bring all of us up to speed on what we have. But first, the word from the pathologist. You'll all be getting her official written report as soon as she can do it, but for the moment, Dr Kirtle has the impression that our killer is a very controlled person. Fastidious was a word she used. He – or she – is also strong enough to cut through muscle and bone to get the heads off. The fact that both bodies were dealt with in exactly the same way, the electrical tape, the knife our killer used, makes me think there's some sort of ritualistic aspect to what he does. But that's just speculation at the moment. Mac, why don't you go through what we know.'

Tennyson nodded and stepped forward to the whiteboards that he had set up earlier. They were adorned with photographs of the two victims, the sites of the killings, maps, and random words written in marker pens.

As Mac began his briefing, Georgiou looked around the room at the rest of his team. Conway, looking far too big for the plastic chair he was sitting on, with an intensity in the expression on his face as he studied the information on the boards.

Sitting next to Conway was DS Debby Seward. Thirty-one years old. Like Conway, a physical exercise nut. Tall and thin, her red hair cropped short, she kept herself fit by weekly visits to the gym and martial arts training at one of the many martial arts schools in Carlisle. Like Conway, she was single. 'Married to the job', as some people put it.

Georgiou had also heard whispers about 'Debby the Dyke', but in his opinion this was only from disgruntled male officers who hadn't been able to get to first base with her. As he looked at her, he remembered how she had been with him soon after Susannah died: soft, caring. There had been a look in her eyes that had even suggested . . .

He shook the thought away. It had been a long time ago, but the pain was like yesterday. Seward was just being sympathetic. 'I'll be there for you, any time night or day,' she'd said, and she'd held his hand. He'd just nodded, given her hand a squeeze back, and then changed the subject. He'd been hardly able to talk about Susannah at that time without wanting to hit something, or burst into tears. Since then Seward had been polite with him, and him with her. She'd never repeated her invitation to him; and he'd never asked her about it. It had been another time. Things had been different then. And maybe it had been his imagination. Just sympathy, one human being to another. But there'd been no whisper of any man in her life. Maybe she *was* gay? Anyway, her private life was her own. So she was single; so was Conway, and no one had ever accused Conway of being gay. At least, not to his face.

Next to Seward sat DC Kirsty Taggart, the other Scot on his team. Thirty-three, married, no children. Small and big-boned, which made her appear plump and slow to people who didn't know her. But Georgiou knew that Taggart could move fast when the situation called for it. Georgiou had seen her disarm a man with a machete just by using a nearby chair, her movements so fast that the knifeman had hardly seen the chair before it hit him.

Next to Taggart was the final member of his team, DC Richard Little, thirty years old, small, quiet, thoughtful, neat and tidy almost to the point of obsession. As Georgiou watched him now, Little was flicking a tiny speck of dust from the leg of his trousers. Georgiou had visited Little at home, and discovered that Little's wife, Vera, was exactly the same. Their house was immaculate inside and out: the front lawn kept firmly cut, the flower borders neat, the house inside orderly with everything in its allotted place. It was not a house where Georgiou had felt comfortable; he'd felt that he was messing the place up just by being there. But Little was a key part of his team with his obsession over making sure every tiny fact was taken note of, every detail was recorded. Fastidious and close attention to detail, that was Little. The very words Dr Kirtle had used to describe the killer.

We're looking for someone like Little, thought Georgiou.

At the boards, Tennyson pointed to one of the photographs on the board, that of a middle-aged woman. It had obviously been taken from police files.

'Let's start with the first one,' he said. 'Victim number one. Michelle Mary Nixon. Age forty. Married twice. Last divorced in 1998. Lived alone in a flat in Haltwhistle just over the border in Northumberland. Two convictions for soliciting. Also on record are charges for drunk and disorderly, and wilful obstruction. Although these charges were later dropped because witnesses didn't want to give evidence. Apparently Michelle Mary was a real tearaway.'

'Children?'

'Three. Two boys and a girl, aged fifteen, twelve and ten.

All in care.'

'A completely different kettle of fish to what we know of Tamara Armstrong,' commented Seward. 'Young, from a wealthy family.'

'Maybe Tamara was a hooker on the side?' suggested Taggart.

'If so, she wasn't very successful at it,' put in Georgiou. 'Dr Kirtle says she was still a virgin.'

'Now there's a rarity in this day and age,' said Conway.

Tennyson pointed to a photo of a small industrial building.

'Michelle Nixon's body was found inside this shed close to the railway line, just outside Haltwhistle.'

'That suggests we're talking local knowledge,' mused Seward. 'Unless whoever did it took a chance.'

'Maybe,' said Georgiou. 'Means of death?'

'Strangled,' said Tennyson. 'Possibly with a length of wire, according to the report. Her head was cut off after she was dead. The body, still clothed, was hanging from a girder, tied with electrical wire around the ankles. All the blood had been drained from the body and had stained the ground beneath her, just like with our one. The head was missing.'

'And no sign of anything sexual?' asked Georgiou.

'No, which is unusual in Michelle Mary's case if it was someone who was a client. Which brings us,' said Tennyson, moving back to the most recent photographs, 'to yesterday morning and the discovery of Cumbria's victim, Tamara Armstrong. Student. Daughter of Edward Armstrong, chairman of the Police Authority.'

Tennyson pointed at a series of photographs of Tamara

Armstrong's body hanging upside-down from a tree. She was fully clothed. Scene-of-crime tape could be seen in the photos. Some were long shots, some close-up.

'Same MO as the one at Haltwhistle,' announced Tennyson. 'Body hung upside-down, this time from a tree. Ankles tied to a branch with electrical wire. Body fully clothed. The area beneath the body was soaked with blood. The body was found by a man walking his dog.'

'Any semen stains?' asked Seward.

Tennyson shook his head.

'No. Just like the other one. If he's doing it to get his rocks off, he's doing that somewhere else.'

'Unless it's a woman who's doing it?' put in Taggart.

'Oh, come on!' snorted Tennyson derisively. 'Each of them was hung upside-down, from a point six feet off the ground in Tamara's case, nearly seven feet off the ground in Mary Nixon's. That means physical strength. I know what Dr Kirtle says, but I don't fancy a woman for it, not without an accomplice.'

'No?' said Taggart archly. She gave a sly smile. 'Have you seen the muscles on some of these women athletes? The shot putters and javelin throwers?'

'Think we ought to round up a few women athletes, chief?' cracked Conway.

Georgiou shot him a frown.

'Sorry,' Conway said ruefully.

'Right, at first sight, what's the connection?' Georgiou asked the team.

'The victims are both women,' said Seward.

'The method? The equipment?'

'An electrician who hates prostitutes and students,' muttered Conway.

'And who collects heads,' muttered Seward.

'There's got to be a link somewhere,' mused Georgiou. 'We know this is the same killer, unless someone did a copycat with the second one.'

'Too many details the same,' said Little. 'The small details that weren't in the press reports.'

'I agree,' said Georgiou. 'So, it's the same killer. Debby and Kirsty, I want you to build up a file on Tamara Armstrong: activities, friends, enemies, where she used to go, what she used to do, clubs, interests, everything.'

'Right, boss.' Seward nodded.

'Richard and Iain, I want you to go through the case file on Michelle Nixon. Then I want you all to cross-check both files, see if there is anything, however remote, that connects the two women. People they knew in common. Places they went to. Maybe hairdressers. Hospital appointments. Regular train journeys. Anything, no matter how small. Let's meet back here at three o'clock this afternoon and check through what we've got. OK?'

'Right, chief,' said Conway, and he and Little, and Seward and Taggart gathered up their notebooks and headed for the door.

Georgiou turned to Tennyson and said: 'Mac, get on to uniform and start them knocking on every door in the roads that lead to the park in Stanwix. I want to know everything everyone saw between midnight and when the body was discovered yesterday morning, no matter how small and apparently insignificant.'

'All in hand, boss,' said Tennyson. 'I put that in motion yesterday.'

'Good,' said Georgiou. 'In that case, you're with me.'

'Right. What are we going to do?'

'We're going to the scene of the latest murder. See if there's anything to give us an idea of what this is all about.'

SEVEN

Debby Seward and Kirsty Taggart had compiled a list of the people that Tamara Armstrong had been out with on the night she was murdered. There were three: Donna Evans, Suzie Starr and Rena Matlock, all girls of about the same age, all former schoolfriends of the victim. They were talking to Rena Matlock now, in the living room of her parents' home in Cavendish Terrace, less than two miles from where Tamara's body had been found.

The house was large, double-fronted, early 1930s, in one of the most exclusive roads in Carlisle, and both Seward and Taggart were aware they were dealing with money. It was in the way that Rena stood by the window while Seward and Taggart sat, as if Rena owned the world and everything in it. Surly, thought Seward. Superior. To her, we're her servants. It's the way she's been brought up.

Their questions had been gentle, probing without appearing to. Georgiou had taught them that: 'Our job isn't to talk, our job is to listen. Let them talk. If they're guilty, they'll say something that will trip them up. If they're innocent but they've got information that can help us, they'll reveal it. But only if *they* talk.'

Rena Matlock was talking now.

'We were in Razza's bar. It's a new one opened in town, at the top end of the town, not far from the Lanes. Do you know it?'

Seward and Taggart nodded.

'We were supposed to be having a girls' night out, just the four of us, but Donna picked up a guy and went off with him at half past ten. She is such a slut! That left me, Suzie and Tamara. We stayed there till just after midnight when Razza's closes. We decided to walk home because our houses are so near, and I don't trust some of the taxi drivers who work late. Some of them are such low-lifes.'

'Have you or any of the other girls had trouble with taxi drivers before, late at night?' asked Taggart.

'Well . . . yes and no,' said Rena. 'They don't actually say anything, it's just the way they look at you. They leer. You know they're trying to hit on you.'

Perhaps if you wore more clothes when you went out at night they mightn't leer so much, thought Seward. She'd seen the way so many of these young girls walked about at night, even in the coldest weather, with skirts that hardly covered their behinds and off-the-shoulder tops that barely hung below their nipples.

'So you walked home,' prompted Taggart.

'Right.' Rena nodded. 'We walked over the bridge, then Suzie went off first because she lives just along Brampton Road. Me and Tamara walked up to Cavendish Terrace and I turned off and walked home. Tamara headed up Scotland Street. She lives . . . lived . . . at Knowefield.'

Suddenly Rena moved away from the window, her fists clenched.

'It could have been me!' she stormed angrily. 'Do you know that! It could have been me!'

Seward and Taggart exchanged looks. Beneath their bland, concerned looks, both knew what the other was thinking: Rena was a spoilt brat who was more worried about what had almost happened to *her* rather than what had happened to someone she claimed to be her best friend.

'I've got to go to the loo,' snapped Rena, and abruptly left the room.

Seward and Taggart said nothing, just waited. They'd been caught before by people who claimed to be going to the loo, and then hung around outside the door eavesdropping for a second or two, trying to pick up information to help them with their alibi. That's if Rena was a suspect, of course, not just a witness. But then, Seward and Taggart had learnt that everyone was a potential suspect. And the closer they were to the victim, the more of a suspect they became. Lots of relationships had their dark side, something that could trigger sudden violence.

As the two women waited for Rena to come back, Seward looked at her partner and wondered what Taggart really thought of her. She was friendly enough in a casual way, but there was a gulf between them. Not that it was entirely Taggart's fault; Seward knew she didn't let people get to her. She also knew that some of the male officers called her a lesbian behind her back, and wondered if it coloured Taggart's attitude towards her. Did Taggart expect Seward to make a move on her while they were out in the car together? If so, she'd be relieved to know that women weren't her thing. Or maybe she'd be disappointed. Who knows which way people swung. OK, Taggart was married, but in her experience that didn't mean much.

The truth was that Seward had a secret: Andreas Georgiou. She'd fallen hook, line and sinker for him soon after she joined his team, a year before. His wife had been alive then. Then his wife had died, and Seward had let Georgiou know that if he wanted to talk, she was there for him. But she hadn't overdone it, just kept it casual, businesslike. Possibly she'd been too businesslike, too casual. He'd just nodded, said 'Thanks', and that was it. He didn't know how she felt, how she'd always feel. She'd thought about coming out and telling him, maybe when they'd all had a bit too much to drink, blame it on the alcohol, but it hadn't happened.

They heard footsteps outside, and then Rena swept into the room. She still looked angry.

'Going back to what you said: you think this was just random?' asked Taggart. 'You don't think Tamara was the deliberate target?'

'Why should she be?' demanded Rena. 'She doesn't mix with the sort of lunatics who'd do this mad thing!' Then she stopped as if a thought had struck her.

'Yes?' Taggart prompted her.

Rena shook her head.

'Even that lot wouldn't do something like this.'

'Which lot?' asked Seward.

'Those creepy geeks she hangs around with from the uni.'

'The Brampton Road campus?' asked Seward.

Rena nodded. 'They make films. Tamara hung around them now and then. I think she wanted to get into films. Be an actress.'

Seward and Taggart exchanged glances. This was an interesting aspect.

'Do you know who in particular she was involved with at the uni?' asked Seward.

Rena shook her head.

'No,' she said. 'I never got involved with them. They're a bunch of fakes. Posers. I warned her against getting involved with them.' Then she frowned. 'Wait, she sometimes talked about someone called Drake.'

'Was Drake his first name or his last name?' asked Seward.

Rena shrugged.

'I don't know,' she said. 'All I know is that Tamara thought he was a genius.' She scowled. 'All these arty types think they're geniuses. I can't stand them.'

'And did she see these people . . . and this Drake . . . a lot?'

Rena shook her head.

'I don't know,' she said. 'I didn't want to know about them.'

'How did she get involved with them?' asked Taggart.

'She just saw them doing some filming in the centre of Carlisle one day and got talking to them. They were making some kind of documentary by the cross in front of the tourist office.' Rena gave a sour little laugh. 'If Tamara saw anyone with a movie camera she'd start talking to them. She was a complete geek like that. Starstruck. I told her, most of these people are sleazy and undesirable and to be avoided.'

'How closely did she get involved?'

'I don't know.' Rena shrugged. 'She didn't talk about them to me because she knew what I thought about them.'

'Except for this person called Drake,' probed Seward gently.

Rena nodded.

'And she only mentioned him to me once. She shut up when I told her what I thought about these so-called artist geniuses. They all die in poverty. What's the point of that?'

The crime scene was a mess. Tyre tracks and footprints on the grass around the tree where Tamara Armstrong had been found hanging. The grass beneath the tree was still stained, the red of Tamara's blood now turning brown. The ground felt spongy beneath Georgiou's feet.

Bunches of flowers had been laid at the base of the tree, bearing cards with messages like 'You were an angel'.

'Check the cards on the flowers,' said Georgiou. 'See if we can trace who left them. Maybe chummy left one, just to be funny.'

Tennyson nodded.

'There's not much here, guv,' he said. 'Tyre tracks from the vehicles that came to take the body away, footprints from uniform.'

'Did you see it before it was messed up?'

'Yes and no,' said Tennyson. 'Uniform were on to it first, then I gather there were a load of ghouls turned up to look. Uniform kept them away and put up screens, but that meant them walking all over the place.'

Georgiou looked at the tree where Tamara Armstrong

had hung upside-down while her killer cut her head off, and at the patch of dried blood beneath. This was the big difference with the murder of Michelle Nixon. Michelle had been murdered and her head cut off indoors, in a railway shed, out of sight of prying eyes. Tamara Armstrong had been killed and her head cut off here in the open, even though it had been in the darkness of the early hours of the morning. Anyone could have come by. What had caused the change in the MO? Maybe the killer needed more of a thrill? The chance of being caught? Like people who got an extra kick out of having sex in public places, doing it without being caught. Maybe it was a challenge, a gauntlet thrown down to the police. See, I kill right out in the open and you can't catch me.

Oh yes I will, Georgiou promised himself grimly.

EIGHT

Seward took a swig from the small plastic bottle of water and then put it back in the glove compartment of the car. God, it was hot! The water had been cold when she bought it an hour ago, now it was already lukewarm. She wondered if she ought to invest in one of those iced water bottles she'd seen advertised in the papers, a padded bottle holder with an ice cube in the bottom. No, she decided, she'd only forget to put it in the freezer every night.

Beside her, in the parked car, Taggart was listening on her mobile, nodding and saying 'Got it' every now and then. Finally she said, 'I owe you one, Nick.' Then she hung up.

Seward looked at her inquisitively.

'A pal of mine,' said Kirsty. 'He teaches creative writing at the uni. A good guy.'

'Does he know Drake?'

'Not well,' said Kirsty. 'A different department. Enough to know his first name though. Eric Drake. Nick says he's a bit of a poser.'

'An opinion shared by Rena Matlock,' commented Seward.

'No, Rena said that everyone at the uni's a poser,' Taggart

corrected her. 'Not true. Take Nick, for example. Like I say, a good guy. Genuine.'

When she saw Seward looking at her with a curious expression, Taggart laughed out loud.

'Nothing like that! I'm a married woman!'

Seward shrugged. 'I didn't say anything,' she said.

'Anyway, if we can't get hold of Drake, Nick suggests we talk to someone called Paul Morrison. He's an occasional lecturer in film at the place. Nick says he's the guy who has most to do with Drake. Today is one of the days when Morrison is in, lecturing.' Kirsty grinned. 'Nick also says Morrison is a pretentious wanker.'

DC Conway looked at the pile of papers in front of him and shook his head. Social Services reports. Charge sheets. Medical reports. He groaned.

Little looked up from his own paperwork and shot a glance at him.

'What's up?' he asked.

'Michelle bloody Nixon,' groaned Conway. 'A complete nightmare. Thank God I didn't live next door to her. Punters. Drugs. Violent and abusive when drunk, which was most of the time. Apart from her being a woman, there is absolutely nothing here which links her in any way to Tamara Armstrong.'

'The names?' murmured Little.

Conway looked at Little and frowned. 'Michelle and Tamara?'

Little shook his head. Then, almost as if he was embarrassed by it, he said: 'Nixon and Armstrong.'

Conway frowned. 'What about them?' he asked.

'They're Reiver names,' he explained.

'So what?' said Conway, shrugging. 'Half the people in the Carlisle phone book have got Reiver names. Graham. Armstrong. Nixon.'

'And Little,' added Little. 'That's what made me think of it.'

Conway shook his head.

'This case is hard enough without bringing the bloody Border Reivers into it.'

Conway remembered being taught about the Border Reivers at school in 'local history'. The Border Reivers were the families who lived in what was known as the Debateable Lands, on the border between England and Scotland between the 1200s and the sixteenth century. It had been a time when there was no law and order in the border region between England and Scotland, and the Reiver families had taken advantage of it. For hundreds of years they lived by robbing on both sides of the border. English or Scottish, it didn't matter. The most notorious were the Armstrongs, the Nixons, the Grahams, the Littles and the Bells. They plundered, murdered and raped, and no one could touch them. Not until James VI of Scotland became James I of England, and he took a hard line with them. He had them rounded up and hanged without trial. It had been known as Jeddart Justice. Those who weren't killed on the spot were given a choice: execution or exile. A lot of them chose exile.

'I don't see it,' said Conway. 'The Reivers died out.'

'Their families didn't,' pointed out Little. 'You said it yourself, just look in the local phone book and see how many people have Reiver names. Thousands.'

'So you're saying this is a family feud from six hundred years ago? That after all this time someone's decided to take revenge and start cutting some heads off? Or maybe it's a ghost coming back and cutting heads off. Like in that film, *Highlander.*'

Little looked at the disbelief on Conway's face, heard the sarcasm in his voice, and sighed ruefully.

'OK,' he said. 'But it's the only thing I can see that connects the two women in any way at all.'

'Maybe that's the point,' said Conway. 'Maybe chummy chose them because they *were* completely different.' He looked at the papers in front of him and let out a long and agonized sigh. 'In which case, us doing this is a complete and utter waste of time.'

Seward and Taggart parked outside the large 1960s building in Brampton Road that housed the University of Cumbria and walked into reception, making their way through a crowd of students who were either soaking up the summer sun or taking a chance to smoke a cigarette. As the uni buildings were strictly non-smoking, and as many of the students looked like they'd be at home in a vampire movie, with their death-white skin and black clothes, Seward guessed it was the latter.

At the reception desk, they asked to speak to Eric Drake.

'I'm sorry,' said the receptionist apologetically. 'I don't think he's in today.' She frowned, and then added: 'In fact I don't think he's been in for the past few days.'

'You know him, then?' asked Seward.

'Oh yes,' replied the receptionist, smiling. 'Everyone knows Drake.'

'In what way?' asked Taggart.

The receptionist seemed to suddenly realize that these two women were officials of sorts, and she suddenly clammed up.

'Nothing,' she said. 'I just meant that he's well known.'

'He must be,' said Seward, 'if you can remember him out of the hundreds of students here and know that he isn't in.'

The receptionist looked momentarily flustered.

'In that case, can we speak to Paul Morrison?' asked Taggart.

The receptionist studied them carefully, aware now that something was up.

'Who shall I say wants him?' she asked.

'Just tell him it's the police,' said Taggart.

The receptionist picked up the phone, tapped out an extension, and then said, 'Is Paul Morrison there? It's reception.' She waited a moment while someone obviously went to call the lecturer to the phone, then she said, 'Mr Morrison? There are two police officers here to see you.' A pause, then she added, 'No, they didn't say what it was about.'

She nodded, then hung up and told them, 'He's on his way down.' Then she added with a sigh: 'It makes a change being able to get hold of him. Usually with these lecturers they're either teaching, or out.'

'Then it's a good omen,' said Taggart, smiling.

They moved aside from the reception desk to wait, and a few moments later a man appeared, out of breath and looking worried. He went to the reception desk, and the woman behind the desk indicated Seward and Taggart.

'Paul Morrison,' he introduced himself, his tone whining as well as slightly aggressive. 'Look, if it's about my car tax, I've already told your office this is a matter of civil liberties—'

Paul Morrison was a short, balding man in his forties, with three earrings in his left ear and two in his right. What little hair he had was pulled back into a ponytail. He was wearing a striped suit and sunglasses. Seward wasn't sure if Morrison was going for the Hip Film Guy look or the Second-Rate Gangster. Whichever it was, at first sight she agreed with Taggart's friend's description of him: a pretentious wanker.

'No,' said Seward abruptly, cutting him off, 'this is about one of your students. Eric Drake.'

'What about him?' asked Morrison suspiciously. 'Who are you?'

Both Seward and Taggart showed him their IDs and introduced themselves.

'Perhaps if we can go somewhere more private to talk?' suggested Taggart. She had already picked up Seward's tone and had immediately switched to 'nice cop' to Seward's 'hard cop'. 'Your room?'

'I don't have a room,' snapped Morrison angrily. 'I'm only a part-time lecturer and so I suffer accordingly. Absolute victimization. This is a truly dreadful place as far as trying to get one's own space. You wouldn't believe it! We're even forced to share lecture rooms.' He looked towards the refectory. 'We could always go in there and talk. Have a cup of coffee while we're doing it.'

Seward looked through the glass doors of the refectory. It was filled with students.

'We'd prefer to go somewhere where we can't be overheard,' she said.

'In that case, the only place is outside,' said Morrison. 'Fortunately today is sunny.' As he led the way outside, he was still complaining. 'It's an outrageous way to treat professional people, not giving them their own space.'

Seward thought about their own cramped and shared offices at police HQ and was going to add a soured comment of her own, but decided against it. She wanted Morrison to be the one who talked.

They found a spot in the grounds away from the groups of students, and Taggart said: 'We'd like to get in touch with Eric Drake.'

'Yes, you said,' said Morrison, nodding. 'Why?'

'It's to do with an ongoing investigation,' said Taggart.

'What investigation?' persisted Morrison.

'I'm afraid we're not at liberty to divulge that at this moment, sir,' Taggart told him. 'However, we understand that Eric Drake isn't in today. Is that right?'

'This isn't a school, Sergeant. It's a university,' snapped Morrison. 'We encourage mature individual creativity, and sometimes the creative mind doesn't conform to the office hours mentality.'

'So any of your students can not turn up and no one bothers?' asked Seward.

'They turn up for lectures, tutorials, that sort of thing, but much of their work is carried out on their own at their own speed.'

'So Eric Drake hasn't had any lectures or tutorials scheduled for the last few days?'

Morrison looked uncomfortable.

'Well, he *has*,' he said, a defensive tone creeping into his voice. Then he looked at Seward defiantly. 'But I'm sure that when he presents the piece he's working on, it will justify the time he has spent working on it outside the campus.'

'And what piece of work is he involved with at the moment?' asked Taggart, trying to put a friendly tone in her voice to counter Seward's aggressiveness. Nice cop, nasty cop.

'Many different pieces of work,' said Morrison vaguely. 'This is not a restrictive course. The students have to complete a wide range of assignments.'

'But what particular piece of work were you referring to when you said that when he presents it, it will justify the time he's spent working on it?' persisted Seward.

'It's a film,' said Morrison. 'A short film.'

'What sort of film?' asked Seward. 'Documentary? Drama?'

'Drama,' said Morrison.

'Any particular genre?' Seward pressed. 'Fantasy? Horror? Film noir?'

Taggart looked at Seward in momentary surprise; then recovered herself. She'd been taken aback to hear Seward talking like one of these art critics on the telly. Morrison also looked at Seward with a new wariness. He checked Seward's expression for any sign of sarcasm, but saw none. The truth was that Debby Seward loved films. She had spent her childhood being taken to the cinema by her father, a complete movie nut, and had come to share his love of films. Laurel and Hardy silents. Musicals. Westerns. She particularly liked old black and white thrillers. Film noir, the film buffs called them. She loved them for the stories, for the intrigue. But most of all for the flawed heroes: the Robert Mitchum types, doing their best to be heroic against a tide of sleaze and corruption.

And, as deeply as she loved film, she had contempt for those who lived off it without giving anything back. Film critics who felt themselves so clever by writing a few witty lines, words which in some cases had destroyed the career of a writer or director or actor. The fakes who couldn't make it as creative people in their own right, so they got their rocks off attacking those who could. People like Paul Morrison.

'I believe Drake's work touches on all known genres,' said Morrison. 'He is a very talented and driven young man. He has a fierce imagination, and a wonderful eye. Do you know the work of Orson Welles?'

The patronizing way that Morrison emphasized the name 'Orson Welles', as if talking to an idiot, prompted Seward to ask 'Do you mean *Citizen Kane* or his television adverts for sherry?' just to annoy him, but instead she just nodded, watching him.

'Drake has the same kind of intensity and individuality about his film-making that Welles had, before the studio system destroyed him,' said Morrison. 'If he can cope with the system, he has a real future in front of him. I believe he has the potential to be another Scorsese.'

'Or maybe even another Curtiz,' said Seward quietly.

Morrison stared at Seward, stunned.

'What?' he said.

'Michael Curtiz,' said Seward. 'The man who directed *Casablanca, Angels with Dirty Faces, The Adventures of Robin Hood*—'

Morrison snapped out of his state of shock.

'I know who Michael Curtiz is, Sergeant!' he said, almost angrily. 'I lecture on film.'

Seward nodded.

'Of course you do,' she said. 'Well, thank you for your time, Mr Morrison. You have been most helpful.'

As the two detectives walked away from Morrison, heading for the car park, Taggart asked: 'What was all that about this Curtiz character?'

'Hungarian-born film director,' said Seward. 'Worked with all the greats: Humphrey Bogart, James Cagney, John Wayne. He directed the only good film Elvis Presley ever made: *King Creole.*'

Taggart gaped at Seward, open-mouthed.

'I like films,' explained Seward. 'When I see anything good, I want to know who made it so I can watch out for their stuff again.' She shrugged. 'I shouldn't have said anything to him.'

'Yes, you should,' said Taggart. 'He was being a pompous prick. You put him down nicely.'

'But I did it because I was angry,' said Seward. 'I got annoyed because he was treating us like morons, like an inferior species because he thinks we don't understand the world of arts, as if he and his kind are some sort of superior species to the rest of the world. I just wanted to put him right. It was stupid. It brought me down to his level.'

'Now who's being superior?' said Taggart, grinning.

They entered the reception area and headed for the desk.

'Right,' said Taggart, ' let's see if we can get an address for this reincarnation of Orson Welles.'

Five to three in the afternoon. At the police station it was time for a pooling of information gathered, if any.

As Georgiou and Tennyson walked past the reception desk on their way to the briefing room, they were stopped by a shout from Sergeant Graham.

'Inspector!' he called.

'What now?' groaned Georgiou, expecting it to be something to do with the superintendent.

As Georgiou approached the desk, Sergeant Graham held out a copy of the local newspaper to him, with a grin.

'Late edition of the *News and Star*,' he said jovially. 'Thought you might like to see what they're saying about you.'

'Let me guess,' hazarded Georgiou. 'That I'm a wonderful human being.'

Graham laughed.

'Not exactly,' he said. 'They've got an interview with Mrs Parks. She seems a bit upset.'

Georgiou shrugged.

'I'll get one later,' he said.

'Take this one,' said Graham, thrusting it towards Georgiou. 'Why waste your money. Let the chief pay for it.'

Georgiou took the paper with a slight grin and went back to where Tennyson was waiting for him.

'Made the gossip columns?' asked Tennyson, grinning.

'Something like that,' said Georgiou.

'What's it say?'

'Let's get our priorities right,' said Georgiou. 'First let's see what everyone else has got, then I'll read my press notices.'

NINE

Seward, Taggart, Conway and Little were all gathered around an open copy of the *News and Star* as Georgiou and Tennyson walked into the briefing room.

'This is crap!' Conway was snorting indignantly. 'Absolute crap!'

'I'm sure it is,' said Georgiou, 'and I'll read all about it later.' He brandished the copy of the paper he'd just picked up from the sergeant.

'Take my advice, don't bother,' said Seward, her face showing she was angry. She moved away from the others and sat down at her desk, still fuming.

'Don't let it get to you,' said Georgiou.

'But you haven't read what Mrs Parks says about you!' protested Conway. 'It's libel! You ought to sue her!'

'No, it won't be,' said Georgiou. 'It will be very carefully phrased, with no direct accusations, just hints and innuendos.'

'Not this one,' said Conway, tapping the open paper. 'She says you beat her son up and it's a disgrace you've been allowed back.'

Georgiou shrugged.

'Like I said, I'll read it later and decide what action to take, if any. In the meantime, let's get back to the priority: the murders. What have you got?'

Ruefully, Conway and Little repeated what they'd turned up, which was just a rehash of what Tennyson had reported at the morning's briefing. Then Seward and Taggart gave their report about what Rena Matlock had said about Eric Drake, and Tamara Armstrong being involved with making a film with him; and their interview with Paul Morrison.

Georgiou nodded, interested.

'This Drake character sounds interesting,' he said. 'The killings have got all the hallmarks of some cheap horror film. Maybe there's something there.'

'Do you want to talk to him?' asked Seward.

'No,' he said. 'You've got it this far. You go with it. So, what else? Any connections between the two women?'

The four detectives looked gloomy as they shook their heads.

'Nothing,' said Conway. 'We've tried everything you suggested, plus a few more. Different hairdressers, different hospitals for their appointments. They lived completely different lives. Nothing at all.'

'Except for the fact they were killed,' said Taggart.

'And their names,' said Little.

There was a pause in the room, and everyone turned to look at Little, who suddenly looked embarrassed.

'Sorry,' he said. 'It's nothing.'

'No, nothing is what we've got,' corrected Georgiou. 'What's this about their names?'

Little looked at Conway, who shrugged as if to say 'This is nothing to do with me'.

'Armstrong and Nixon are both Reiver names,' said Little.

And, with a shamefaced look that told everyone perhaps he felt he was being foolish, he enlarged on what he'd said to Conway about the Reivers being the connection. When he had finished, he looked around at the others.

'Well,' he said defensively, 'we were asked if we knew of a connection.'

'True,' said Georgiou. 'And, however far-fetched, at the moment it's the only one we've got. OK, leave that one with me. For the rest, Seward and Taggart, go and dig out this Drake character. Conway and Little, go and see if forensics have finished their report yet. I want everything. What was under Tamara's fingernails. Any traces of chemicals or anything on her skin. The killer must have gripped her to tie her up; let's see if he left anything at all. Traces of deodorant. Sweat. Hairs. Anything. Where did the electric tape come from? Let's nail down absolutely everything.'

'Got it.' Conway nodded. As the big Scot got up, he picked up the copy of the newspaper. 'You sure you don't want this?' he asked.

Georgiou shook his head.

'I said, I've got one.'

'Yes, but you might want two copies,' said Conway. 'One to throw darts at; one to keep and read later when you're calm.'

Georgiou smiled.

'I'm already calm,' he said.

As the four detectives left the room, Tennyson turned to Georgiou.

'So, what's our next move, boss?' he asked.

'We're going to see a historian and talk about the Reivers,' said Georgiou.

TEN

Georgiou and Tennyson were sitting in the office of Diane Moody, one of the curators at Tullie House Museum, listening to a lecture on headhunters given with great enthusiasm for her subject. Diane Moody was a large woman with enormous, powerful-looking hands. Strangler's hands, thought Tennyson.

'As I have said, you will find the cult of the headhunter all over the world,' Moody told them. 'I've already given you the example of the jungles of Borneo, but in other parts of south-east Asia . . .'

'I was thinking more of it being found in Britain,' said Georgiou gently. 'Historically speaking, that is.'

'Of course.' Moody nodded. 'Forgive me. I tend to get carried away. Well, it did happen here, obviously. Mainly among the Celts.'

'The Celts?' asked Georgiou.

Moody nodded again.

'As I'm sure you know, Inspector, at the time the Romans arrived to occupy Britain, the dominant peoples here were the Celts. It is generally reckoned they had come here from continental Europe, particularly Gaul. Now, of course, France.'

Georgiou nodded to show that he was following her.

'The Celts spread across Britain, into Wales, up into Scotland and, of course, Ireland, the three countries that still retain a great deal of Celtic culture. Not least in their language. Gaelic in Ireland and Gallic, spelt Gaelic but pronounced Gallic, in Scotland.'

Georgiou nodded again.

'And the heads?' he asked gently, before this developed into a full-blown history of the Gaelic-speaking peoples of the world.

'You know that this area was settled by the Brigante tribe of Celts when the Romans arrived?' she said.

I do now, thought Georgiou. He decided if he said 'No', he and Tennyson would just get a big lecture on the sub-cultures of the Celtic tribes in northern Britain, so instead he just nodded and gestured for Moody to continue.

'The Brigantes, along with the other Celtic tribes, believed that if they took the heads of their enemy, they would at the same time be taking their power. So, the more heads they collected, the more powerful they became.'

'What did they do with the heads once they'd collected them?' asked Tennyson.

'They built them into the walls of their encampments. Again, the same phenomena can be found in parts of south-east Asia. Walls built of human skulls. I find it fascinating that cultures so far apart geographically are so close culturally. Don't you, Inspector?'

'I do indeed, Ms Moody,' agreed Georgiou. 'What about

the Border Reivers?'

'Ah.' Moody beamed happily. 'Now that's a different topic altogether, and one on which Tullie House has an enormous amount of material. Another fascinating phenomenon: a culture of family lawlessness which has echoes on the other side of the globe, notably in Canada and parts of middle America. Although that could be, of course, because so many Scots were exiled to North America, either through poverty or punishment. Did you know that when the Americans landed on the moon in 1969, the three men who stood on the podium at the big celebrations were all from Reiver families? Neil Armstrong, the astronaut, Richard Nixon, the President, and Billy Graham, the church leader. History follows us through time!'

'But did they collect heads?'

Moody looked at him and frowned.

'Heads?' she repeated. 'The Border Reivers?'

'Yes,' said Georgiou.

Moody shook her head.

'Good heavens, no,' she said. 'Head collecting is associated with pagan religions. The Reivers were Christians. Well, at least nominally. The image of the Christian religion is the Hanged God, not the beheaded one. Are you familiar with Frazer?'

'Which Frazer would that be?' asked Tennyson.

'Sir James George Frazer,' said Moody. 'The Golden Bough.'

Georgiou shot a quick glance at Tennyson and saw that his sergeant looked as bewildered as he did. Moody spotted this and went on to explain.

'The first volume was published in 1890 and it's never been out of print. It is the classic study of magic and religion.'

'I see,' murmured Georgiou. 'When were the Reivers operating again?'

'I think I can safely say the organized lawlessness that one associates with the Reiver families first came to notice in the middle of the thirteenth century,' said Moody. 'The Law of the Marches was introduced in 1249 to try and bring order to the region. These attempts failed, of course, because the border area was so far from the two seats of government for the two countries of England and Scotland. Certainly the Reivers became stronger and stronger during the 1300s and 1400s, but it was during the sixteenth century, the 1500s, that Reiver activity reached its peak.'

'But if a Reiver was caught, he was executed?' asked Georgiou.

'On rare occasions,' agreed Moody. 'Generally the officers of the law ransomed them back to their families. Most law officers at that time were as crooked as the thieves they were supposed to catch.'

'But if they were executed,' persisted Georgiou, 'how was it done? I remember that Henry VIII had the heads of his wives chopped off. And Mary Queen of Scots was also executed the same way. Did that happen to the Reivers who were executed?'

Moody shook her head.

'Execution by axe was for the upper classes only,' she said. 'Criminals, and that certainly included the Reivers, was by hanging.'

As Georgiou and Tennyson walked back to their car, Tennyson broke into a chuckle.

'What a history lesson!' he laughed. 'I learnt more in twenty minutes with her than I did all the time I was at school.'

'But does it help us?' asked Georgiou. 'If she's right, we have to go even further back in history than the Border Reivers to find the motive of our killer. Back to the Celts.'

Tennyson shook his head.

'Sorry, boss, I don't buy it,' he said.

'You don't?' asked Georgiou..

'No,' said Tennyson. 'I think all that does is complicate things unnecessarily. What we've got is two women murdered. One old, one young, but both women. That's the common link. We're looking for someone who hates women.'

'And the heads?'

Tennyson shrugged.

'OK, maybe he collects them. But not because of anything that happened in history. They're tokens. Killers and rapists do it all the time, take something from their victims as a memento.'

'It's one thing taking a watch or locket or a mobile phone, it's another thing entirely to cut off someone's head and take it away,' said Georgiou. 'Think about it, Mac. Our killer is *very* methodical. The way he did them, there's almost a kind of ritual in the way the bodies were hung up.'

'They were hung up to let the blood drain out.'

'But the way the wires were tied. Everything exactly the same. It feels like some kind of ritual. What the actual ritual is, or what it's based on, we don't yet know, but I think we're looking for someone who likes ritual. And every ritual has a root in history.'

Tennyson shook his head.

'Sorry, guv,' he said. 'It seems much simpler than that to me. He does it the same way because it works. It's that simple.'

Georgiou sighed.

'You may be right,' he said. 'Maybe I'm seeing too much into this. Anyway, let's take a break today. I promised Ted Armstrong I'd go and see him and let him know what we've got.'

'Which is nothing,' said Tennyson.

'True,' admitted Georgiou. 'But we're filling in the details. Something will pop up. We're going to get him, Mac. Trust me.'

ELEVEN

Georgiou arrived at the large double-fronted house in Stanwix, where the Armstrongs lived, just after six. His ring at the doorbell was answered by Ted Armstrong. The man looked deathly pale, as if the blood had been drained out of him and only about half the amount had been put back. There were deep lines on his face, grey shadows beneath his eyes.

'What have you got?' he asked.

'Not a lot at the moment,' said Georgiou. 'Is this a bad time? Maybe if I came back later?'

'It's always going to be a bad time from now on,' said Armstrong.

He opened the door wider and Georgiou stepped in.

Sophie Armstrong was sitting on a settee as Georgiou followed Ted Armstrong into the large palatial living room. It had a gold look to it. Gold ornaments on shelves and hanging on the walls, among the paintings. Reproduction classic French furniture: settees and chaise longues with gold upholstery. It was all ostentatious, a way of showing off the fact that Ted Armstrong had gone from nothing to one of the wealthiest men in the city. But now, the overwhelming feeling in this room was pain. It was in the way that Ted Armstrong held himself, like a marionette struggling to stay upright after its strings had been cut. And it was written all over Sophie Armstrong. Georgiou had only met her a couple of times before, at official police functions. Then he had thought she looked a very well-preserved forty, possibly could even pass for thirty. Now, looking at her, drawn and haggard and with her make-up badly applied, she looked more like sixty.

Georgiou spent an uncomfortable half-hour with the Armstrongs. There was nothing he could tell them, and they knew it. All he could do was be with them and try and share their grief for a short while.

Georgiou was glad of the drive back home to Bowness. Driving along the road across the marsh, with the Solway Firth stretching away to Scotland, and the vast expanse of sky overhead, it helped wash away the city. Carlisle was only small, but every city had a feeling of intensity about it. It was the closeness of the buildings to one another, the crowds of people pushing and shoving, the traffic. Carlisle was better than most, but Georgiou knew he could never live in a city again. He needed the feeling of space that the expanses of the Solway Plain gave him. Sea and sky.

That evening, as he ate a supper of pasta he prepared for himself, he finally got down to reading the article in the *News and Star*. There was nothing new. But that was because there was nothing new to say. The allegations, however, were there in black and white in Mrs Parks's words: 'He beat up my son and they're letting him get away with it because he's a copper. He's a vicious thug and he ought to be locked up.'

Georgiou wondered if they had been deliberately provocative in the hope that he would sue for libel. If so, they were mistaken. In Georgiou's opinion, the only people who got rich from libel were lawyers. No, the real thing that annoyed him about this case was the fact that Ian Parks was still walking around free, and his supporters, including Councillor Maitland, seemed to be succeeding to a certain degree in their campaign to depict him as the victim of the case.

Georgiou put the paper aside and sat down with a writing pad and started to jot notes down about what they knew so far about the killer of Tamara Armstrong and Michelle Nixon. It was a thing he did when he had a problem to unscramble, whether it was a particularly difficult crossword, or a case. Put the random thoughts down in a seemingly meaningless way, and sometimes the answer would just pop out at him. He looked at the words he had written down:

Electric flex. Broad bladed knife. Heads taken. Border Reivers. Head cult. Pagans. Celts. Ritual? Butchery skills. Stanwix. Haltwhistle. Railway shed. Park. Strong wrists. Strong enough to lift body into position. How tall is killer? Fastidious. Neat and tidy. Clothes splashed with blood. No sex. Gloves. Transport for killer? Michelle – prostitute. Drinker. Tamara – virgin. Michelle hanging from girder. Tamara hanging from tree. Eric Drake. Film. Horror? Paul Morrison. Diane Moody. Strong hands. Razza's bar. Rena Matlock. Donna Evans. Suzie Starr. Ted Armstrong.

Chairman of Police Authority.

He sat for a while, looking at the words, but nothing leapt out at him. It was there, he could feel it. Somewhere in those words was the answer, if only he could find the connection.

Maybe if he went to the pub he might find the answer forming in his brain. Sometimes, if he had a problem he couldn't solve, he'd go to the Kings Arms, the only pub in the village, and sit and talk to his friend and neighbour, Denis. Denis's farm was about five miles outside the village, but he also had a small cottage in the village a few doors away from Georgiou's house. A bachelor, Denis would often leave his farm in the charge of a nephew and head for the Kings Arms of an evening, where he would sup a few pints and talk to anyone who was in before heading for his small cottage for a few hours then heading back to his farm in time for early milking. He and Georgiou never discussed any of the cases Georgiou was working on; their talk was usually about local issues, farming issues, the fortunes of Carlisle United, other football issues, and the politics of the world. Ecology, the environment, the world economy, nationalism, individualism: you name it, Denis would be able to talk about it. And talk about it knowledgeably and objectively, not just rant from one viewpoint as so many people did.

And sometimes, as Georgiou and Denis talked, randomly and wide-ranging, a little spark would be set off, a crack in the mystery of whatever was puzzling Georgiou over his latest case.

He looked at the disjointed list he'd written. Maybe tomorrow he'd talk to Denis. Maybe tomorrow he'd crack the puzzle over a pint. Right now, he was tired. The visit to the

Armstrongs had drained him. The pain on Ted and Sophie's faces. All that grieving. It had been like looking in a mirror.

He sighed. Maybe tomorrow. Now, it was time to sleep on everything.

The ringing of the phone beside his bed cut through Georgiou's sleep. As he struggled to sit up, his eye caught the clock by his bed. Four o'clock. A phone call at four o'clock in the morning always meant trouble. He snatched up the receiver.

'Georgiou,' he grunted.

'Duty Sergeant Sims,' said a voice. 'Sorry to wake you up, Inspector, but there's been another one. Dead body, hung upside-down, head missing. Thought I'd better let you know at once.'

Georgiou was already getting out of bed.

'You did the right thing,' he said. 'I'm on my way.'

TWELVE

It was lucky it was summertime, thought Georgiou, otherwise we'd need the big lights at this time of the morning, and that would be a big part of our annual budget gone. But here in mid-June in north Cumbria, a quarter to five in the morning was broad daylight. He parked his car by the other police cars and headed for the walls surrounding the old Roman fort of Birdoswald.

A uniformed officer hurried towards him. Georgiou recognized him as Sergeant Filby. He'd worked briefly with him in the past, but not enough to say he knew him well.

The body was still in place, hanging upside-down from a wooden beam set in a stone archway. Georgiou was glad to see the area around the body had been taped off by SOCO, keeping casual visitors at bay. From this distance Georgiou could see that the body was fully clothed, this time in jacket and trousers.

'Same MO as the others, sir,' said Filby. 'The head's missing. The wrists and ankles have been tied with electrical wire.'

'Do we know who it is?'

'Not yet. It's a man, but I didn't want to start rummaging around in his clothes looking for identification until you got here.'

'Good thinking,' said Georgiou approvingly. 'Are the scientific team here?'

'On their way,' said Filby. 'I contacted them the same time as I got in touch with you. I've also had the area roped off where there are tyre tracks, just in case it's our man.'

'Good,' said Georgiou again.

This was the way he liked it. Keep a crime scene intact until every inch had been explored, every fibre picked up, every piece of evidence extracted.

'Who discovered the body?'

'A man out walking his dog.'

Another early-morning dog walker, thought Georgiou. He was surprised by the fact that the victim was a man this time. Why had the killer changed his or her pattern? The theory that the killer hated women had just gone out of the window.

'Guv!'

He turned and saw Mac Tennyson heading towards him. Behind Tennyson the scientific team had just arrived and were unloading their equipment from their vehicles. Things were happening.

Tennyson looked rough, like he'd just been dragged out of bed. Which, indeed, he had.

'I would have been here earlier but the traffic lights on Wigton Road had got stuck on red. Traffic chaos.'

'Chaos?' queried Georgiou.

'Well, three cars backed up waiting for them to change. In

the end I just went through them. Thought I'd let you know in case you get a complaint.'

Tennyson gestured towards the taped-off scene..

'What's the score?' Tennyson asked.

'Exactly the same as the others, except this one's male,' said Georgiou.

'Oh?' Tennyson frowned. 'Why?'

'Exactly my question,' said Georgiou. 'We'll let the science team do their bit, then we'll go and see what we can work out.'

Tennyson looked around the area surrounding the remains of the Roman fort, at the open landscape, the nearby road.

'Out in the open,' he commented. 'First in Stanwix, now here. He's taking a chance, isn't he?'

'I think it's a way of boasting on his part,' said Georgiou. 'A challenge. Each time he's pushing the boundary further. I wonder what next?'

'A body hanging up in the middle of Hardwicke Circus?' suggested Tennyson.

At the mention of Carlisle's most notorious traffic bottleneck, the huge roundabout that fed the traffic between England and Scotland, Georgiou shuddered.

'Don't even joke about it,' he said. 'Anyway, while the science guys are still busy, let's get on the phone and tell the rest of the team, and tell them we want them in for a briefing on the latest killing.'

'OK, guv,' said Tennyson, pulling out his mobile. 'What time do you want them in?'

Georgiou looked at his watch and made a quick

calculation. Say another hour for the science teams, then an hour for himself and Tennyson to go over the spot and give orders to uniformed.

'Tell them eight o'clock,' he said. 'And tell them they're lucky to be having a lie-in, unlike us.'

THIRTEEN

Eight o'clock, and the team were assembled in the briefing room: Mac Tennyson, Debby Seward, Kirsty Taggart, Iain Conway. Only Richard Little was missing. Conway had phoned his home and Little's wife had said she'd pass on the message, but so far there was nothing from him. Georgiou couldn't wait for him; Little would get the information later.

'As you all know, there's been another killing,' he told them. 'The body was found at the old Roman fort at Birdoswald. Same MO as the other two. Body strung up. Head cut off and removed. This time the victim was a man. From identification on the body, he appears to be a Chinese takeaway owner from Carlisle called Han Sun, so I think we can forget the Border Reivers link . . . unless there was a Chinese branch of the Reivers that we don't know about.'

A new section of evidence boards had been set up, these devoted to information on the latest killing. So far all that had been put up were photographs of the scene of the crime. The rest were blanks to be filled in.

'We need answers: What was Mr Han Sun doing at

Birdoswald? Did our killer meet him there, or take him there? Conway, pick up Richard and then I want the pair of you to go and see the victim's family and his workmates. Everyone who knew him. Let's try and piece together the last time anyone saw him.'

'Right, boss,' said Conway.

'Seward and Taggart, I think it's time you had a word with this Drake character.'

'Right,' said Seward.

'Uniform are still going over the site at Birdoswald, so we'll let them get on with that. Mac and I will stay here and co-ordinate things, pick up any information we can. Keep your mobiles switched on so we can get hold of you if anything turns up.'

The address they'd been given for Eric Drake was a house in Denton Holme. It was one of the larger houses, and had all the hallmarks of student occupation: the curtains at some of the windows were closed, others had been replaced with a sheet hanging down, partly shielding the occupants of the room from prying eyes. They were responsible, though: in the small area at the front of the house one wheelie bin had a homemade label stuck on it which said 'Can recyling'. Taggart lifted the lid and revealed a bin filled to the top with empty beer cans.

'Any bets they're all male students?' she said as she shut the lid.

'You think women students don't drink beer?' asked Seward.

'Not this much,' said Taggart.

She rang the bell, and after a moment the door was opened by a bleary-eyed young man of about twenty in jeans, T-short, bare feet, and a woolly hat.

'Yeah?' he asked.

Taggart and Seward showed him their police ID.

'Police,' said Seward. 'Is Eric Drake in?'

The young man seemed to be struggling with this sudden appearance of the police on his doorstep, and whatever was going on in the house.

'What time is it?' he asked.

'Our question was first,' said Taggart. 'May we come in?'

'Er . . .' began the youth.

'Thank you,' said Taggart, and she and Seward stepped inside. There was the definite smell of cannabis clinging to the inside of the house.

The youth looked at them, unhappy.

'Shouldn't you have a warrant?' he demanded.

'That depends if you've got anything to hide,' said Taggart. 'Have you?'

'No,' said the youth defensively.

'Fine,' said Taggart. 'So, where can we find Eric Drake?'

'He's . . . he's still in bed.'

'Then I'm sure he won't mind us calling on him,' said Taggart. 'Where's his room?'

The youth hesitated.

'Of course, we could always go knocking on all the doors and look for him,' said Taggart. 'Who knows what we might find?'

The thought of the two policewomen searching through the different rooms in the house made his mind up for him.

'Top of the stairs. Second door on the right. It's got an Iron Maiden poster on it.'

It would have, thought Seward. Heavy metal, another of her pet dislikes. What with that and a would-be career as a pretentious film director, she was beginning to dislike this Drake character more and more before she'd even met him.

The door to Drake's room was easily found. It wasn't just the Iron Maiden poster pinned to it, it was also the gothic graffiti that adorned the rest of the door.

Seward knocked. There was the sound of a grunting from inside.

'That sounded to me like "Come in",' commented Taggart.

'That's what I heard as well,' agreed Seward.

The door was unlocked, and as they pushed it open the rank smells of sweaty, unwashed clothes and stale tobacco came out and hit them. The room was in darkness, the thick curtains pulled shut. Taggart switched on the light, although a shawl had been thrown over the shade of the central light, so that even with the light on, the room still seemed to be dark.

The mess in the room was a sight to behold. Leftovers of meals on dirty plates on the floor. Beer cans. Ashtrays overflowing. Clothes crumpled and just discarded, hiding most of the floor and what furniture there was in the room.

There came more grunting from the bed at one side of the room, and then a tousled head poked itself out from under the covers, like a tortoise coming out of hibernation.

Eric Drake squinted at the two women.

'What the f—' he began. 'Who are you?'

'Police,' said Taggart, and once again she and Seward

held out their police IDs. 'Are you Eric Drake?'

'No,' said the young man.

Seward and Taggart exchanged looks.

'In that case, would you get dressed? We'll need to talk to you down at the station.'

'What? Why?'

'Because you're in Eric Drake's room and we wish to find out where he is.'

There was a pause, then the young man in the bed asked, 'Why?'

Taggart and Seward had adjusted their vision to the gloom and saw now that the man in the bed was in his late twenties, with long, greasy hair and the beginnings of a beard. Or perhaps he just hadn't shaved for a few days.

Seward sighed. 'Look, can we cut all this,' she said. 'All we want to do is ask you some questions about a film you're making. Then we can get out of here.'

At the mention of his film, Drake sat up in the bed.

'What about my film?' he demanded.

'First, what did Tamara Armstrong have to do with it?'

Drake looked puzzled.

'Tamara?' he asked. 'You mean the girl who was killed?'

'That's exactly who we mean,' said Seward. 'We understand she was in your film.'

'No way!' said Drake vehemently. 'I use proper actors.'

'So what was her part?' asked Seward. 'Crew? Background artiste?'

'Yeah.' Drake nodded. 'Background artiste. An extra.' Looking from Seward to Taggart and back again, he appealed: 'Look, can we do this downstairs so I can get a coffee? I've only just woken up.'

'Here is fine,' said Seward. 'This way we don't have an audience. Or, if you prefer, we can do it at the station?'

Drake shook his head.

'Here is good,' he agreed with a sigh. 'What do you want to know?'

'For a start, your movements on the night Tamara was murdered.'

Drake looked at them, his mouth hanging open in shock.

'You think I'm a *suspect*?' he said.

'At this moment we're asking this same question of everyone who knew Tamara to help eliminate them from the enquiry,' said Taggart. 'So, could you give us details of your movements on the night in question?'

'When was it?' asked Drake.

Seward thought that Drake looked as if he would have difficulty remembering what had happened to him a few hours ago, let alone some days before. But then, that could be a clever ploy. Drake thought for a bit, then he began his story. According to Drake they'd held a party at the house on the night Tamara Armstrong had been murdered. Tamara Armstrong had not been amongst those invited. Taggart took down a list of names that Drake gave them as having been at the party. According to Drake, he hadn't left the house at all that night; or the next day until about three in the afternoon to go and buy some milk and cigarettes.

After the practicalities were out of the way, with names, addresses and mobile numbers of the people Drake claimed were his witnesses, Seward switched the subject back to the film.

'What's it about, this film of yours?' she asked.

'Pagan sacrifice,' said Drake.

'What sort of sacrifice?' asked Taggart. 'Cutting people's heads off?'

Drake shook his head. 'Being eaten by crows,' he said.

'Crows?' echoed Taggart.

'I wanted to do a big burning thing. Like in *The Wicker Man*. But there's these fascists in Health and Safety who say you need all sorts of licences. So instead I'm going for crows.'

'How does the sacrifice work?' asked Seward.

'The victim is laid out in the middle of a stone circle. We're using Castlerigg outside Keswick. You know it?'

Seward and Taggart nodded.

'The victim has honey and stuff smeared on her eyes and throat, and the crows come down and peck her eyes and throat out. It's like symbolic.'

'Aren't crows difficult to train to do that sort of thing?'

Drake smiled, smugly.

'Tight close-ups. Lots of cutaways,' he said. 'No one uses real birds.'

'Hitchcock did,' said Seward. 'They drew blood from Tippi Hedren when he was shooting *The Birds*.'

'Yeah, but Hitchcock was a control freak,' said Drake. 'He had a thing about tormenting blonde women.' Taggart gave Seward a look of appeal that said: 'Can we finish this before he starts giving us a lecture about his favourite film directors, and you join in with him?'

'Have you got a copy of the script?' asked Seward.

'Why?' asked Drake. 'You need it for some sort of evidence? Everything I've said is the truth. It's crows.'

'We'd still like to see a copy of the script,' insisted Seward.

Drake shrugged, and then hauled himself out of bed, revealing a pair of loose underpants. He went over to the table, cleared some clothes off it, and produced a few typewritten pages stapled together.

'Here,' he said. 'I was looking at it last night because we start filming in a couple of days. I want the ambience to be right for it when we're at Castlerigg, so we're doing it on June 21st. The Summer Solstice.'

As he handed the script to Seward, he told her warningly, 'This is copyright, you know. I don't want anyone ripping it off.'

'Trust me, I'm a police officer,' said Seward, straight-faced.

Once they were back outside the house, Taggart took a long, deep breath.

'At last, I can breathe again!' she said.

Seward smiled.

'I know the feeling,' she said. 'I feel like we ought to spray ourselves with disinfectant. One thing's for sure: if our murderer is, and I quote, 'fastidious and organized', then it certainly isn't our friend Drake.'

As the two women walked back to their car, Taggart asked, curious: 'What did you want a copy of his script for? It's gonna be crap.'

'Maybe,' said Seward. 'But, like I said, I'm a film nut. And who knows what interesting things it might tell us.'

FOURTEEN

Georgiou and Tennyson were in the office, going through the initial reports from SOCO and uniformed division on the Han Sun murder, when Georgiou's phone rang.

'Georgiou,' he said into the mouthpiece.

It was Superintendent Stokes. 'I need to see you,' he said, his anger obvious in his tone. 'My office, immediately.'

There was a click as the phone disconnected.

Tennyson gave Georgiou an enquiring look.

'Our lord and master,' grunted Georgiou. 'Stokes has summoned me.'

'A promotion?' suggested Tennyson sarcastically.

Georgiou laughed. 'I'll be back as soon as I can persuade him we're doing all we can,' he said.

With that Georgiou headed out of the room and up the stairs.

Stokes was pacing as Georgiou walked into his office. Before Georgiou could speak, Stokes turned on him, furious.

'I've just had New York on the phone to me. *New York!*'

Georgiou frowned, puzzled.

'I'm sorry, sir, I don't see what we have to do with New

York,' he said.

'The press, Georgiou!' raged Stokes. 'As if it isn't bad enough being under siege from the British media, now the world's press have got hold of it! "Head Killer!" That's what the headlines say. Not just here but in New York! Three murders, Georgiou! Three!'

'With respect, sir . . .' began Georgiou.

'No!' thundered Stokes. 'No respect at all, because this murderer has none! Certainly none for us! He's making you look a laughing stock!'

'With respect, sir,' continued Georgiou firmly, 'I only came back to work yesterday morning.'

That made Stokes stop whatever was on the tip of his tongue, but only for a moment. He continued pacing, agitated.

'In all my long career I've never had anything like this. Never! My position is being questioned!'

And not before time, thought Georgiou.

'And this business in the *News and Star* about you doesn't help!' snapped Stokes. He took a deep breath, then turned to Georgiou. 'I think, in fairness to this department, you ought to consider your position, Inspector.'

A cold chill went up Georgiou's spine.

'Consider my position?' he repeated. 'Do you mean resign?'

Stokes turned away, unable to meet Georgiou's look.

'You know what I mean!' he blustered. 'Your actions over this boy—'

'Unproven allegations,' interrupted Georgiou.

'And your appalling lack of success over these murders,' continued Stokes, as if he hadn't heard Georgiou's comment, 'have brought discredit on this force.'

'I repeat,' snapped Georgiou, even more firmly than before, 'I only returned to work yesterday. Now if you want me to make a statement to the press stating my position, and the difficulties that I have been placed under which hamper my investigation . . .'

Stokes stared at Georgiou, open-mouthed.

'What difficulties?' he demanded.

'The false allegations against me, the lack of support from superior officers . . .'

Stokes's mouth shut like a trap, and he glared at Georgiou.

'How dare you!' he challenged. Then he swung away and thought for a moment, before turning back to Georgiou. 'Under no circumstances will you talk to the press. Not one word.'

The phone on Stokes's desk rang and he snatched it up.

'I told you I was not to be disturbed!' he barked angrily. Abruptly his manner changed, and he said apologetically: 'Of course. You did the right thing. Put him through.'

Someone important, thought Georgiou.

'Yes, sir,' he said, his tone respectful, but at the same time breezy and confident. He listened briefly, nodding the whole while, then continued: 'Actually, Inspector Georgiou is with me at the moment . . .' Then suddenly he stopped, his face going white. It was as if someone had punched him in the stomach. 'Of course, sir. What was that website again?' He grabbed up a pen and scribbled a note on a pad. 'Yes, I'll go onto it straight away, and if it *is* terrorists . . .' He listened again, still nodding, and then said: 'I'll get back to you immediately, sir.'

As Stokes hung up, Georgiou asked, 'Terrorists?'

Stokes didn't reply; he was too busy tapping keys on his computer, an expression of urgency on his face. An image appeared on his screen, a figure wearing what looked like a shapeless smock and a hood over his or her face with eyeholes cut in. As Stokes turned up the volume, Georgiou heard the voice, a young man's, ranting.

'These deaths are the price the ungodly will pay!' he shouted, his voice muffled by the hood but still audible. 'An eye for an eye! A tooth for a tooth! A head for a head!'

Stokes stared at the screen, his face ashen.

'It *is* terrorists!' he said, shocked. He turned to Georgiou. 'These killings are being done because of some Jihad, or whatever it is they call it! It's Al-Qaeda!'

'Not necessarily,' said Georgiou. He pointed at the screen. 'Look at the symbols in the background. That one's an ankh.'

'What the hell's an ankh?' demanded Stokes, bewildered.

'It's an Egyptian symbol,' said Georgiou.

'Egyptians!' exploded Stokes. 'Muslims!'

'No,' said Georgiou firmly. 'The ankh is from ancient Egypt, predating most conventional religions. It's found mostly these days in fantasy games, or as a fashion decoration.'

'So what are you saying?' demanded Stokes.

'I'm saying this doesn't look to me like Islamic terrorists.'

'So who is he? Could he still be our murderer?'

'Yes,' admitted Georgiou. 'Or he could be just some loner jumping on the bandwagon.'

'The press will have a field day with this!' groaned

Stokes. 'You have to sort it out, Georgiou. Find out who this character is.'

'I think that might be a job for GCHQ, sir,' said Georgiou. 'And then the Terrorist Squad.'

'You said you didn't think he was a terrorist!' said Stokes.

'I said he doesn't look like or use the same language as an *Islamic* terrorist,' countered Georgiou. 'At least, not the ones we've seen broadcasting their demands on TV and the web.'

'Yes, well, I guess you'd know, if anyone,' sighed Stokes.

'I beg your pardon?' asked Georgiou, irritated.

'Well, with your background. The Middle East.'

'My background is London,' said Georgiou firmly.

'Yes, well,' said Stokes uncomfortably. 'The point is that was the chief constable on the phone and he's worried how this is going to turn out. If this is a terrorist plot we'll be right in the firing line! The press. Politicians. Demonstrations!' He glared accusingly at the phone on his desk and growled, 'New York will be just the start of it!'

FIFTEEN

Iain Conway sat in the small room above the Chinese takeaway, his notebook open on his lap, pen in hand, nodding and making notes as Mrs Sun poured out her grief. The shop was in Botchergate, not far from the railway station, in a long street filled with pubs and other takeaways of all sorts: Chinese, Indian, Turkish, Greek, as well as a plethora of burger bars, all selling the same rehashed meat under a variety of names: Mexican Burger, Burger-Q, New York Burger.

The pubs and bars along the street offered the same variety: an Australian bar, an English bar, a Scottish bar. A serious drinker could sup the whole of the United Nations in a pub crawl along Botchergate, interspersed with munching on indigestible so-called international cuisine, most of which tasted the same: burger and chips. With or without mayo or sauce.

Han Sun Chinese takeaway was the same as most along the street: a takeaway at the front opening on to the pavement, with a cramped kitchen behind. And, above, a tiny cramped flat which housed the Sun family: the late Mr

Sun and his wife, Mrs Sun's younger sister, May, and Mrs Sun's two brothers, Mr Li Key and Mr Li Chan. There was no sign of any children in this room or elsewhere in the flat, or any clues that children lived here: no toys, no comics.

Conway nodded intently as he listened to them talk. Mainly it was Mr Li Chan, the elder of the two brothers, who did the talking. He was talking now, while Mrs Sun cried and her sister hugged her to her, doing her best to comfort her. Mr Li was talking angrily about racist attacks they'd suffered. He seemed sure that the killing and beheading of Mr Sun was an extension of these racist attacks.

'We come to this country, work hard, pay taxes, and they spit at us. Break our windows!' said Li. 'We call police! Police do nothing!'

'We're not sure if there's a racist motive behind this dreadful crime,' said Conway, choosing his words carefully. 'The method seems to have been the same as in two other recent cases, but both of those were English people.'

Mr Li shook his head angrily.

'This racist!' he insisted. 'Who else want kill my brother-in-law? He good man. Have no enemies. Always pay taxes. Pay bills on time. He gentle. Everyone like him.'

At this, Mrs Sun wailed again and began crying loudly and painfully. Her sister threw her arms around her and hugged her close, letting the widow sob into her. So much pain, thought Conway. So much grief. And we get it all the time. No one ever hears good news from us. It's always: 'I'm afraid I've got some bad news. Your husband, wife, son, daughter, has been killed.' And then the face looking out from the doorway would fall, the tears would start.

Sometimes they'd faint. At least this time, the family had already been given the bad news and Conway was there to fill in the details of Mr Sun's life, and what he might have been doing near Birdoswald at midnight.

'He not go there,' said Mr Li, again shaking his head firmly. 'Racists take him there and kill him.'

'What racists?' asked Conway.

'Racists who break our windows. Shop windows,' he added. And then, in case Conway had forgotten, he repeated: 'We tell police.'

Conway made a note to check with HQ as to when these attacks on the Suns' takeaway had been carried out, and whether there'd been any progress in finding the culprits. He doubted it. There'd been a rise in racist attacks lately, mainly against Pakistani-owned shops and businesses. Or, rather, against business owned by people that these racists *thought* were Pakistani. Which meant that Indians, Burmese, Sikhs, Greeks, Turks, even some darker-skinned Spaniards, had been attacked under the mistaken belief that they were supporters of Islamic fundamentalism, and so responsible for attacks on British troops in Afghanistan. Racists and bigots weren't noted for their intelligence, reflected Conway. And that extended to his own countrymen and the outbreaks of violence whenever Rangers and Celtic played in an Old Firm game. Protestant and Catholic. The Union Jack and the green, white and gold of the Irish flag. Broken bottles and knives. God save us from the mindless havoc of bigots and racists, thought Conway ruefully.

He stayed for another half-hour, filling his notebook with details about Mr Sun's last hours, and then, after once more offering his condolences, walked down the narrow stairs to Botchergate. As he reached the street, his mobile rang.

'Conway,' he said.

'Tennyson,' said the DS. 'Something's come up. The boss wants everyone back here for a meeting, so if you and Richard can get here as quick as you can, that will be very much appreciated.'

'No problem,' said Conway. 'I'm just in Botchergate. I'll be there in five minutes.'

He hung up, and frowned. That was one question that really puzzled him: where was Richard Little? When he'd called at the Littles' house that morning, Vera had told him that Richard was 'still at work'. This puzzled Conway. What work? Did Richard have another job at night, a moonlight? Richard had never mentioned anything about such a thing to him. And there'd been something in Vera's manner that had been odd. Furtive. She'd been pleasant enough to Conway when she opened the door to him, but there had been something else behind her plastic smile: tension. She looked worried.

Something's wrong, thought Conway. It could be that Richard and Vera were having problems. If so, he wondered whether he should say anything to Georgiou. Georgiou would certainly wonder where Richard was. Whatever was going on, one thing Conway knew was that Richard wasn't 'at work'. Tennyson had said for him *and* Richard to get back to HQ. So if Richard wasn't at work, and he wasn't at home, where was he?

Maybe Vera had just been lying, and Richard was at home, but hadn't wanted to show himself. Maybe that's why

Vera's manner had been so shifty. But, if that was the case, surely Vera would have come up with a better excuse than 'he's still at work'. She'd have said that Richard was ill in bed at home, asleep, or something. Or maybe 'being at work' was just the first excuse to come into her head.

He thought it through. Vera was shifty. Maybe lying. Lately, Richard had been acting oddly. Tense. Tired, as if he hadn't been sleeping properly. All of which suggested that there was something not right between Richard and Vera. But *if* Richard and Vera were having personal problems, that was their business. Conway was sure that Richard wouldn't thank him for bringing their boss into it. For the moment, the best thing was to keep a low profile on it.

The rest of the team were already assembled when Conway walked into the briefing room. Seward, Taggart and Tennyson were clustered around a laptop, studying the screen, while Georgiou stood behind them, pointing at different parts of it. Georgiou look at Conway as he joined them, an inquisitive frown on his face.

'Where's Little?' he asked.

'I couldn't get hold of him,' said Conway.

Georgiou frowned.

'Why? Wasn't he at home?'

'No,' said Conway. 'I tried his mobile as well, but he's not answering.'

'That's not like him,' said Georgiou.

'It's possibly nothing,' said Conway, keen to move off the topic. But, knowing that Georgiou wouldn't let the subject rest, he added reluctantly: 'It's just a hunch, but I get the

impression things may not be right between him and Vera.'
He knew that anything else he said would just raise further,
and more awkward, questions about Richard.

'Marriage!' snorted Tennyson.

'Let's leave that for the moment,' said Georgiou, cutting
off further discussion about the pros and cons of marriage
before Taggart could rise to the bait. He pointed at the
computer screen. 'Right now we've got a PR problem to deal
with because it's giving our lord and master upstairs, and
his lord and master, the chief constable, panic attacks.'

'Worse than three headless bodies?' asked Conway.

'Yes,' said Georgiou. 'Take a look.'

Conway stepped forward and looked at the figure on the
screen: the shapeless smock, the hood, heard the ranting
voice, and he drew in his breath sharply.

'I don't believe it!' he said, awed. 'Not Al-Qaeda claiming
these!'

'That's what Superintendent Stokes seems worried about.
And the chief constable,' muttered Georgiou. 'But take a
closer look.'

Seward and Taggart moved their chairs to one side so
that the big Scot could get a better look at the screen.

'That's an ankh,' he commented, pointing to the shape
that Georgiou had earlier identified to Stokes. He frowned,
pointing at another. 'And that's a swastika. Or, almost a
swastika.'

'The original swastika symbol,' said Taggart. 'I did
symbols for one of my modules on my OU degree. The
swastika was a symbol denoting Shakti in Indian religions.
Hindu or Buddhist. It was only turned into a Nazi symbol in

the 1930s.'

Conway frowned. 'So what are we saying?' he asked. 'That this guy's a Nazi?'

'No,' said Taggart. 'If he was, he'd be using the modern version of the swastika, not the ancient Indian one. There are also other symbols in the background. Some are conventional religious symbols, some are pagan or pre-Christian.' She pointed at the screen. 'Those are ancient runes from Scandinavia. And those mixtures of lines in small groups are Ogham.'

'Ogham?' echoed Conway.

'A pre-Christian form of writing,' explained Taggart. 'They were carved into trees or the corners of stones. The lines are symbols, with a different number of lines meaning a different word.'

'Still this OU degree?' asked Conway.

Taggart nodded.

Conway sighed. 'I'm surrounded by intellectuals,' he sighed.

'I haven't finished it,' said Taggart. 'I'm just doing a module now and then, when I can.'

'So, any deductions on this guy?' asked Georgiou.

'A religious nut, but not for any particular religion,' suggested Tennyson. 'Listen to him rant. The only reference to religious is when he says the victims were killed because they were "ungodly". That covers a lot of things.'

'In fact, I'm not sure if it's actually a *religious* nut,' said Taggart thoughtfully. 'There's such a mish-mash of symbols here. It reminds me of those geeks who spend all their time in their bedrooms playing fantasy fighting games on their computers, and give themselves names like WarDeath.'

'But even they sometimes come out of their bedrooms and start killing people,' put in Georgiou thoughtfully.

'Usually with automatic weapons,' added Tennyson.

Conway gestured at the screen.

'So, could he be a suspect?' he asked.

'If he is, hopefully we'll find out soon enough,' said Georgiou. 'I've got GCHQ digging into it to try and trace where the website's coming from.'

'It could be anywhere on the planet,' said Taggart. 'America, Asia, Australia.'

'If that's the case, it means he's not our killer,' observed Tennyson.

'No, but he may be connected to the killer,' said Georgiou. 'An accomplice. The public voice of our secret assassin.'

He pressed the pause button, and they all looked at the shape on the screen, stopped in mid-rant, arms thrown up high.

'There are too many lunatics out there,' sighed Conway. 'Once upon a time they just stayed in their rooms, or walked along the street talking to themselves. Now, with the internet, they have a global audience.' He shook his head. 'Instant uncensored communication! All it does is make a bad world worse!'

'Maybe, but at least you can get the racing results quicker than you used to,' observed Tennyson.

SIXTEEN

The briefing over, Georgiou detailed the team their immediate tasks. Tennyson was told to go to the IT department to try and dig deeper into tracing the website. Seward and Taggart were to continue interviewing everyone in Tamara Armstrong's circle, from a list of names they'd compiled.

'It's going nowhere, boss,' Seward complained.

'Dr Kirtle seemed to think Tamara knew her killer. If we can find any link between Tamara and Michelle Nixon, or Han Sun . . .'

'There isn't one,' said Taggart. 'Not between Tamara Armstrong and Michelle Nixon, anyway. There are no names as a common link. No common group. Neither of them were connected in any way, not socially, not even in the kind of shops they went into, the places they went to, or the magazines they read.'

'Check Tamara out against Han Sun,' said Georgiou. 'Talk to her friends. Find out if she ever went there for a takeaway.'

'It's clutching at straws!' Seward protested.

'Right now, straws are all we've got,' said Georgiou gloomily.

Seward and Taggart nodded, and left, their faces showing they were unconvinced. Georgiou turned to Conway, and for an awful moment Conway thought that Georgiou might be going to ask him about Richard Little, but instead the inspector wanted details of Conway's visit to the Han Sun family, and what he'd been able to find out about Han Sun's last known movements.

Conway told him what he'd learnt: that Han Sun had closed up the takeaway at midnight. Mrs Sun had been upstairs, getting things ready for breakfast for the next morning, waiting for her husband to come up from the shop.

'Her two brothers also live above the takeaway. They share a room. They both work in the kitchens. Mrs Sun's sister works on the counter, along with Mr Sun, the victim. The sister has her own room upstairs, as well.' He gave a sigh. 'It's a *very* crowded flat.'

'Tensions between them?' asked Georgiou.

'Not that I picked up,' said Conway. 'I'm just saying that it's so crowded they don't have any choice but to keep a very close eye on one another.

'Anyway, according to Mr Li Chan, the older brother who does most of the talking, he and his brother and their sister went upstairs to have a late-night drink of tea with Mrs Sun, and then they went to bed, leaving Mrs Sun to wait for her husband. But he never came up.'

Georgiou frowned.

'He never came upstairs?'

Conway nodded. 'That's what they said.'

111

'So they . . . what . . . just went to bed? Didn't anyone go downstairs to the shop to see where he was?'

'Not according to Mr Li,' said Conway. 'I couldn't get much out of Mrs Sun, she doesn't speak much English. Nor does the younger brother. So I got most of this information from Mr Li and Mrs Sun's sister.'

'Doesn't that strike you as odd?' asked Georgiou.

'Not really,' said Conway. 'It often happens that one of a couple goes to bed before the other one, and then falls asleep.'

'So let's look at the scenario,' said Georgiou. 'Mr Sun is downstairs in the shop. It's midnight. He's locked up. Where are the stairs between the shop and the flat? Does he have to leave the takeaway to get up to the flat?'

Conway scanned his notes.

'No,' he said. 'He can do, because there's a separate set of stairs from the street to the flat, with a separate door, so people can go in and out of the flat without going through the shop. But there's another flight of stairs at the back, from the kitchen, that go directly up to the flat.'

'And which flight of stairs does Mr Sun normally use after he's closed up the shop?'

Conway checked his notes again.

'According to Mrs Sun, he uses the stairs from the street,' he said. 'At least, that's what her brother, Mr Li, translated what she said as.'

'Why?' asked Georgiou. 'Think about it, Iain. He's in the shop. He's already locked the door to stop more customers coming in. There's a set of stairs in the kitchen that takes him up to his flat. Why would he bother to unlock the shop, go out into the street, lock the shop door, then unlock the door from the street to go upstairs?' He frowned. 'Did you see where the two sets of stairs came into the upstairs flat?'

'Yes.' Conway nodded.

'Do either of them go straight into one of the bedrooms?'

'No,' said Conway. 'They both came up to a landing.'

'So it's not a case of not using one particular set of stairs because it goes into a personal living space of his brothers-in-law, or his sister-in-law.'

'No,' said Conway, shaking his head.

'So, it's still the same question,' said Georgiou. 'Why does Mr Sun use the stairs from the street rather than from the kitchen?'

Conway shook his head again.

'No idea,' he admitted. 'Do you think that's what happened? That he went outside to go upstairs using the door from the street, and was grabbed by the killer, who then took him to Birdoswald?'

This time it was Georgiou's turn to shake his head.

'No,' he said. 'I think Mr Sun went somewhere else after he finished work for the night.'

Conway looked at him, startled.

'You think he's got a fancy woman?' he asked.

'No,' said Georgiou. 'If my hunch is right, we'll know where he was taken from, and it won't be outside his takeaway.' He picked up his phone, dialled the IT department, and asked to speak to DS Tennyson.

'Mac,' he said. 'I'm going with Conway to have another word with the Sun family. It might be a bit of a delicate chat, so I'm going to keep my mobile switched off so we're not interrupted. If anything comes up, I'll sort it out when we get back. OK?'

'No problem,' said Tennyson.

'How are you getting on with IT?' asked Georgiou.

'Slow,' said Tennyson. 'Slow, but steady.'

'I'll see you when I get back,' said Georgiou.

Conway frowned, puzzled.

'What do you mean, a delicate chat?' he asked.

'I'll tell you if I turn out to be right,' said Georgiou. He stood up. 'OK, let's go and see this Mr Li.'

SEVENTEEN

Georgiou and Conway sat in the same small cramped room above the takeaway where Conway had sat just an hour or so before. This time only Mr Li, the elder of the two brothers-in-law, was in the room with them. Mrs Sun was in her bedroom being comforted by her sister. The younger brother was downstairs in the kitchen of the takeaway, preparing food for that evening. As Mr Li had told them as they sat down: 'Work goes on.'

Georgiou studied Mr Li. He was in his fifties, Georgiou guessed, and with the death of Mr Sun, Mr Li was now the head of the family. Before, Mr Li had just been 'a worker'; the name on the shop front was 'Han Sun Chinese Takeaway', so Mr Sun had been the boss. There was a great deal of wariness in Mr Li's eyes. He wasn't happy about being alone with the two policemen. With his two sisters and his brother in the room, he could hide, divert attention onto many other things, but not alone with these two.

He's wary because he's hiding something, thought Georgiou. And I think I know what it is.

Georgiou offered his condolences again, in a sympathetic

voice, and asked a few mild questions about Mr Sun, rephrasing most of them from those which Conway had asked in his earlier visit, all to lull Mr Li into dropping his guard a bit. It didn't work. Mr Li remained as wary as ever; so Georgiou dropped his bombshell, still keeping his voice low, gentle, concerned, as he asked: 'Where was last night's game?'

Mr Li looked back at him, a puzzled expression on his face, but Georgiou had caught the momentary look of concern in his eyes.

'Game?' repeated Mr Li. He shook his head. 'What game?'

'Mahjong,' said Georgiou. And he added a brief sentence in some strange sounds that caused Conway to look at his boss, taken aback.

Mr Li looked uncomfortable, then shook his head fiercely.

'No game,' he said firmly.

Georgiou leant forward, his face showing concern.

'Mr Li,' he said, 'I'm not interested in causing trouble for people who want to relax after a hard night's work with a friendly game. I'm not interested in illegal gambling—'

'No illegal gambling!' snapped Li sharply.

'All I'm interested in is finding out who killed your brother-in-law. And I think you want that, too.'

'Racists!' barked Li.

Georgiou nodded.

'It may well be racists,' he said. 'But we need to get evidence to find out *who*. And, to do that, we need to know where he was last night so we can examine the area and see if the murderer left any clues when they snatched your brother-in-law. I don't need to see the inside of the place, just the outside. Once I know that, I'll have my men check every inch of the distance between the shop and there, checking for clues. I know it's not far, because your brother-in-law walked there. I know that because we've checked with the taxi companies, and he didn't use a cab. Nor did he take a car. Which means it's not far from here, walking distance. Now, as I say, I'm not interested in arresting anyone for gambling, but if we're going to catch the person who did this to your family, I need to know where to start from. And you're the only one who can help me with that information.'

Georgiou sat watching Mr Li, doing his best to keep the tone of his voice friendly, approachable, unthreatening. Li sat silent, obviously weighing up his options in his mind. Finally, he muttered: 'Tait Street.'

'Thank you,' said Georgiou. 'Which number?'

'Fourteen.'

'And did Mr Sun play there last night?'

Li shook his head.

'I go there and ask. They tell me he not come.'

'So he was snatched somewhere between here and Tait Street,' said Georgiou. 'What time did he leave here?'

'After shop shut and cleared up. One o'clock.'

Georgiou nodded.

'It would take about ten minutes to get to Tait Street. So he was snatched sometime during those ten minutes.' Georgiou got up and held out his hand to Li. 'Thank you, Mr Li. There'll be no trouble for your friends, but I will need to send DS Conway here to talk to them, to confirm what you've told me. I'll give you time to talk to them to reassure them they won't be arrested.' He smiled. 'Not this time, and not by me.'

'Thank you,' said Li, and he took Georgiou's hand and shook it.

As Georgiou and Conway stepped out into the street, Conway asked: 'How did you know? About the gambling? And was that Chinese you were speaking?'

'Cantonese,' said Georgiou. 'And just a brief word or two. While I was in the Met, I did a stint in Chinatown. I learnt two things there. One: if you say a couple of words in Cantonese it worries them into thinking you might know a whole lot more, so they don't use that "No speak English" ploy. Two: once the Chinese restaurants and takeaways close for the night, there's only one game in town for most of the cooks and waiters – gambling – and usually it's mahjong. But mahjong gambling is a very noisy business, those tiles being thrown down makes a hell of a racket, and there's always lots of shouting when players lose. So it would need to be in a house where that kind of noise at night is already going on, and the houses around won't complain.'

'And Tait Street has got quite a few houses with students living in them,' said Conway, nodding. 'Yes.' He turned to Georgiou. 'But you don't think that Mr Li was gambling there?'

'No,' said Georgiou. 'Because if he had been, he'd have been with Han Sun when he was snatched.' He looked along Botchergate towards Tait Street. 'There are CCTV cameras along here, aren't there?' he asked.

'Yes,' said Conway.

'Right. Get along to the council and ask to check the CCTV footage in Tait Street between 1.00 and 1.15 this morning. Let's see what vehicles were around at that time, and run their number plates. Also, get uniform in and get them to check the route between the takeaway and 14 Tait Street; pick up every piece of litter they can find and bag it. It may lead nowhere, but it might give us a start.'

EIGHTEEN

Inside the briefing room at HQ, the phone on Tennyson's desk rang. It was the desk sergeant.

'There's a Diane Moody wants to talk to the inspector. I told her he was out, so she wanted to talk to you. She says she's got some information she thinks you need to know.'

Not more on the Reivers, groaned Tennyson inwardly

'Put her through,' he said.

There was a click, then Diane Moody's voice came through. 'Sergeant Tennyson?'

'Speaking.'

'I think I might be able to throw some light on these murders. Especially after the one that was reported this morning, on the news. It was at Birdoswald, wasn't it?'

'Yes,' said Tennyson.

'Then I definitely have something.'

'And that is. . .?' asked Tennyson, pen poised over his notepad.

'Do you think you could come to Tullie House and I'll explain? It'll be easier than over the phone.'

Warning bells rang in Tennyson's head. More history?

'If you could give me a clue. . . .' he began.

'Or, if you prefer, I could come and see you.'

Tennyson weighed it up. Once she was in the building it might be hard to get rid of her. Diane Moody did love to talk. At least, if he saw her at Tullie House, he could offer an excuse and leave.

'Don't worry,' he said. 'I'll come and see you. I'll be there in about fifteen minutes.'

He hung up and scribbled a note: 'Gone to Tullie House to see Diane Moody. Mac.' He added the time beneath, then placed it on Georgiou's desk.

'Right,' he muttered to himself wearily. 'Time for another history lesson.'

But then another thought occurred to him. Maybe Diane Moody had been in the area of Birdoswald the previous night and had actually seen something. But who goes to a place like Birdoswald in the middle of the night? Tennyson chuckled to himself. Someone who was doing something she'd rather other people didn't find out about. Maybe that was the real reason Diane Moody didn't want to say anything over the phone.

As Georgiou walked back into the office and saw the note from Tennyson, his phone rang. It was the desk sergeant.

'I've just had that woman reporter from the *News and Star* on again, Inspector,' he said. 'Jenny McAndrew. It's the fourth time.'

'I trust you told her I wasn't available,' said Georgiou.

After the report in the paper hinting that he was guilty of beating up an innocent youth, Georgiou had issued an order to his team that no one was to talk to Jenny McAndrew. 'Whatever you say, she'll twist,' he'd told them. 'So if you don't tell her anything she'll have nothing to base her so-called journalism on.'

'I told her, but she said it was important,' said the desk sergeant.

'If she phones again, tell her I'll talk to her when the murder case is solved. Until then, I'm busy. And so are the rest of my team.'

With that Georgiou hung up. He was just sorting through the forensic reports on Tamara Armstrong and Michelle Nixon when his mobile rang.

'Yes?' he said.

'Inspector, you're a hard man to get hold of,' said a woman's voice, and Georgiou recognized it as Jenny McAndrew.

'That's because I'm busy,' he said. 'Might I ask how you got my mobile number?'

'That's privileged information,' she said. 'I need to talk to you about these murders.'

'No comment,' said Georgiou curtly.

'But . . .' began McAndrew.

'All enquiries have to go to press liaison. They'll be able to answer any questions you have.'

With that Georgiou ended the call.

As he expected, his mobile rang again almost immediately. He checked the number. As he expected, it was Jenny McAndrew calling again. He ignored it and let the voicemail pick it up.

He was returning to the reports on Han Sun when his

desk phone rang. At least it won't be Jenny McAndrew, he reflected as he picked it up.

'Georgiou,' he said.

It was a woman's voice. Very young, by the sound of it.

'I've got some information,' she said.

Her voice was muffled, as if she was speaking through cloth of some kind.

'What sort of information?' he asked.

'I can't talk on the phone,' she said. 'Can you meet me?'

'When?' asked Georgiou. 'Where?'

'Do you know the lock-up garages on Raffles? Off Mardale Road?'

'Yes,' said Georgiou.

'I'll see you there in half an hour. Come alone.'

'How will I recognize you?' asked Georgiou.

'I'll know you,' said the voice. 'If you bring anyone, I won't show.' And then the line went dead.

Georgiou rang through to the switchboard.

'I've just had a call,' he said. 'Did you get the number it came from? Was it a mobile?'

There was a pause, then the operator said: 'No. It was public call box.'

'Where?'

Another pause, then the operator said: 'Local. Creighton Avenue.'

The Raffles estate. Which fitted with the location the caller gave.

Georgiou dialled Mac's mobile phone. It was switched off. He left a message telling Mac he was going to the Raffles estate following up some promised information. Then he left.

The chances were it would turn out to be a false errand. But at this stage in the game, with the murderer on the loose, he couldn't afford to turn down any chances.

NINETEEN

Tennyson followed Diane Moody into her office, the same one he and Georgiou had been in the day before.

'Would you like coffee, or tea, or anything?' she asked.

'No, thank you,' he said.

She gestured him to a chair. As he sat down, he said: 'You said on the phone you had information about the latest murder.'

'Not just the latest, all of them,' she said. 'It was when I heard about the latest murder this morning that I understood the connection.'

'The connection?' queried Tennyson.

Moody reached into her bag and took out a map and spread it on the table. Tennyson recognized it as the area between the Solway Firth on the east coast and Newcastle on the west. A line had been marked along it, and on the line three crosses had been made in pen.

'Stanwix, Birdoswald, Haltwhistle,' said Moody, indicating the three crosses.

'Yes?' said Tennyson, none the wiser. The feeling that Diane Moody may have seen something and come in with real and hard evidence was definitely evaporating. It's another history thing after all, he said to himself gloomily.

'They are all the points on Hadrian's Wall.'

'Hadrian's Wall?' repeated Tennyson.

'Yes,' said Moody, nodding. 'Whoever is doing these killings is doing them along the line of Hadrian's Wall.'

Tennyson looked at her, and it struck him that Diane Moody was enjoying this. It was as if this was an academic puzzle to be solved. Then a kind of detective antenna inside Tennyson's head registered that there might be a hint of something else behind Moody's relish. She was treating this like playing a game. Maybe, just maybe, she might be part of the game. Tennyson's eyes were drawn again to Moody's large, strong hands, and now he registered her broad shoulders. Moody could be strong. How strong? Strong enough to hang a body from a tree? Or maybe there was more than one person involved?

'Tell me about Hadrian's Wall,' said Tennyson, and he pulled his chair closer to the desk.

Georgiou pulled his car into the space in front of the lock-up garages that backed onto Mardale Road. Three cars were on the space; two of them with flat tyres. Abandoned, he guessed. A glance at the third showed no tax disc on the windscreen. Stolen, or abandoned, or left to rot.

He sat behind the steering wheel for a moment, waiting and watching. There was no one around. He wondered if she was watching him, whoever she was. If so, where was she?

He got out of his car and looked across the road to the houses on the other side. Neat little houses. Small front lawns kept short and trim. Low fences. One even had window boxes with a display of brightly coloured flowers. He could see a notice on the gate of one of the houses: 'Beware of the dog', with a picture of a fierce-looking Rottweiler. The house next door also had a sign on its gate, but this one read: 'Never mind the dog, beware of the householder.'

Georgiou grinned. He liked odd notices, variations on traditional themes. Like those stickers in the rear windows of cars that instead of saying 'Baby on Board' said 'Beware: Lunatic at the Wheel'. Politically incorrect, and also possibly illegal if the Health and Safety obsessives had their way, but they amused Georgiou.

He guessed that the householders across the road weren't amused by the lock-up garages they looked out on. The large metal doors were covered in graffiti; some of it obscene, some of it intelligible only to local knowledge. 'PT duz it,' said one. Does what? thought Georgiou. Who was PT? Or what? And why spell 'does' as 'duz'? It was the texting generation, writing in some form of abbreviations.

The abandoned cars added to the feeling of run-downness and general depression.

When he first came to Carlisle, his colleagues had warned him about the Raffles estate. They told him it was a no-go area. Dangerous. Many of the houses had been boarded up and used by drug addicts. Needles hidden in the grass and lying on the tarmac were a major hazard. And don't leave your car on the estate, his colleagues had said. They'll have your wheels off and sell them back to you within the hour. Things had changed since then. Many of the old houses had been demolished. Some of the difficult tenants had been removed. The new ones who had taken their place had been vetted, it was claimed. Raffles was going upmarket. But it still had people on it like Ian Parks and his family. They were so firmly entrenched they'd never leave, not unless they were forced out. And with someone like Councillor Maitland protecting them, that was unlikely to happen.

Georgiou looked around. He'd give it five more minutes and then he'd go. No one was around. No one was coming. No, wait! There was someone coming: a young woman wheeling a baby-pusher. Was this her?

Georgiou watched as the woman approached . . . and then she walked straight past.

Georgiou wondered if it was a hoax. A joke of some kind. Bringing him out here in a false errand to waste his time.

He looked at the grassy patch next to the garages. As well as a collection of litter, drink cans, there were two supermarket shopping trolleys and a ripped mattress. He guessed that after dark this patch of land became the gathering place for one of the many gangs of feral youths that haunted the city's estates. And not just the estates: the underpasses, the parks, school yards. It wasn't just in Carlisle, it was a national problem. At least Carlisle didn't suffer from the same levels of gang violence that places like Nottingham and Bristol did. Gun crime. And don't even start me on London and Birmingham and Manchester, he thought. Drive-by shootings. City estates out of control run by gangs of all ages, from old-time thugs down to nine-year-old kids on bikes and drugs. Most of them armed to the teeth.

He looked at his watch. Another eight minutes had

gone by. OK, that was it. A false errand. Or maybe she'd chickened out at the last minute? Whatever it was, if she was genuine, she'd phone again.

He walked back to his car and opened the door. As he was ducking his head down to get in, he sensed rather than saw a movement behind him. He started to turn, but it was too late, something heavy crashed down on the side of his head, and he felt himself tumbling down, banging his face on the bottom of the doorway of his car.

He tied to stagger up, forcing himself out of the car, trying to swing his arms, but something had been dropped over his head, a cloth of some sort. He couldn't see; all he could feel were blows and kicks forcing him down. He tried to tear the cloth off his head, but arms gripped him, pinioning his arms to his sides. Something hit him hard on the head, through the cloth, and he felt sick, felt himself sliding into darkness. . . .

He was aware of the ground hard and cold beneath him. There was the sound of a shout, the thud of feet running away . . . and then Georgiou was falling . . . falling . . . falling. . . .

TWENTY

Tennyson watched Diane Moody as she talked, her large fingers pointing out illustrations in the books she'd taken down from the shelves, and pointing out places on the large map of Britain she'd spread out on her desk.

'But you say the Romans didn't cut off and collect the heads of their enemies,' he queried.

Moody nodded.

'That's right,' she said. 'The head cult was practised by the ancient Britons, as I mentioned before. But there was one noticeable exception: Suetonius Paulinus.'

'Who was. . .?' queried Tennyson.

'Governor of Britain from AD 58 to 61. In AD 61 there was a major uprising by Queen Boudicca against the Roman occupation. An army of 250,000 Britons rose up against the Romans, but Paulinus defeated them with a force of just 10,000 men.'

'And he cut their heads off?'

'No,' said Moody. 'He cut off the heads of his own men on a campaign just prior to this in AD 61, when he drove the Druids out of Anglesey, in north Wales. You see, contrary to general opinion, the majority of the Roman army was not made up of Roman soldiers. Thousands of the troops came from different parts of the Empire: Germany, North Africa, Gaul. And it was the Gauls in one of Paulinus's auxiliary companies that caused him concern when he was preparing to attack the Druids hiding on Anglesey, because many of them still followed the pagan religions of the Celts and believed that the Druids were all powerful. So he had every tenth man in the Gaulish auxiliary beheaded. You may have heard of the word "decimate". That's where it comes from: killing every tenth man in a Roman military unit, as an example to the others. From the Latin 'deci', or tenth. Which, of course, is also where we get the word decimal from.'

'And what happened?' asked Tennyson, intrigued in spite of himself.

'Paulinus led his men across the Menai Strait to Anglesey and they slaughtered every man, woman and child on the island. They also burnt the sacred groves of oak trees to wipe out any trace of the Druids.'

A sudden thought struck Tennyson.

'You said this happened in AD 61?'

'Yes,' said Moody, nodding.

'But the Romans didn't start building Hadrian's Wall until AD 122, sixty years after that.'

'That's right.' Moody nodded again.

'So . . . how is it connected with Hadrian's Wall?'

'In one way it isn't,' admitted Moody. 'But in the cutting off of the heads, it is: either because of the ancient British connection, or the example of Paulinus instilling discipline into his troops by beheading his own men. Either way, these murders have taken place along the line of Hadrian's Wall. Now, that could be coincidence, or it could be deliberate. But if it is deliberate, then I believe you're looking for someone who has an obsession with either the Romans, or the Ancient Britons.'

As Tennyson headed back to his car, he wasn't sure whether he'd just wasted valuable investigating time listening to yet another of Diane Moody's historical lectures, or whether he was on the fringe of putting her in the frame as a suspect. She'd said it herself: they were looking for someone with an obsession with either the Romans, or the Ancient Britons. And that certainly summed up Diane Moody.

He had just reached his car when his mobile rang.

Georgiou was sitting on a bed in the A&E department at Cumberland Infirmary when Tennyson walked in. Georgiou's face looked a mess. There was a livid purplish bruise starting just above his left eye that spread across his forehead, with a gash in the flesh at the centre of it. Another bruise was on his left cheekbone.

'Bloody hell!' said Tennyson.

Georgiou groaned ruefully. 'OK, Mac, you can tell me I was stupid to go there alone,' he said.

Tennyson shook his head.

'Not me, sir,' he said. 'But then, I never contradict a superior officer. If you say you were stupid . . .'

Georgiou tried to get up, then groaned and sat down again.

'The doc thinks they might have broken a rib or two,' he

said. 'We're just waiting for the X-rays to come back.'

'If it's any consolation, we've got one of the bastards,' said Tennyson.

Georgiou looked at him, impressed.

'Already?!' he said.

Tennyson nodded. Then he added: 'Well, we haven't got him *as such*, but we know who he is. His name's Billy Patterson. A local teenage hoodie. He lives on the estate. We were lucky that one of the people who lived opposite the garages saw what was going on, and he recognized him. It seems there were four of them, and they all had hoodies on. But luckily Patterson wears a very distinctive top which he'd painted himself, including misspelling "anachrist" instead of "anarchist". Also his hood fell off at one time during the attack. Luckily for us, the witness is an ex-soldier who says he's fed up with these teenage thugs on the estate – that's why he came forward. We warned him he might be in danger from other thugs for giving evidence, but he just said, "Let 'em try. They know me around here. Anyone messes with me I'll tear their head off."'

'Pity there aren't more like him around,' said Georgiou. 'What's his name?'

'Wilson,' said Tennyson. 'Former sergeant in the Parachute Regiment.'

'Right, remind me to buy former Sergeant Wilson a pint when this is over,' said Georgiou. 'But not before,' he added hastily, seeing the look of concern on Tennyson's face. 'We don't want the defence accusing us of bribing a witness with beer. What's happening about Patterson?'

'Seward and Taggart are on their way to his house to pick

him up.'

'They'll need a search warrant if they want to find this top of his,' said Georgiou. 'Remember what Stokes said: everything by the book.'

Tennyson nodded. 'That's all in hand, guv,' he said. 'They're getting the warrant as we speak.' He sat down next to Georgiou. 'So?' he said. 'Why?'

'This is nothing to do with the murders, Mac,' said Georgiou.

'Ian Parks?'

Georgiou nodded.

'It has to be. Raffles estate. Parks's home territory. ' Ruefully he added: 'And I walked right into it.'

'The question is, can we connect this Billy Patterson to Ian Parks?' said Tennyson. 'You know what that lot are like: they clam up. The threat of a sentence doesn't frighten them because they know it quite likely won't happen, it'll just be a hundred hours' community service, or an Anti-Social Behaviour Order. And these kids treat ASBOs like some kind of badges of honour, proving they're hard nuts. And even if they do get sent down, with fifty per cent remission, plus the time spent on remand, they're out in a month. It's a joke.'

Georgiou nodded.

'I agree,' he said. 'But it's up to us to make that connection. And by the book. Which we'll do once we've got Billy Patterson in custody. So, apart from me getting myself beaten to a pulp, what else is new?'

Tennyson told him about his latest meeting with Diane Moody, and her theory about Hadrian's Wall and the

Romans.

'A little bird nagging at the back of my brain wonders if she mightn't be a bit more involved than she lets on,' he added.

'In what way?'

'Well, for one thing, look at those hands of hers,' said Tennyson. 'If you ask me she's strong enough to do it. And maybe she feels superior to us, all this history stuff she spouts. Maybe she's making fools of us, which is why she's told us about Hadrian's Wall. Making us run around in circles.'

'She kills three people just to make a point about her superior mind?' queried Georgiou.

Tennyson shrugged.

'People have been murdered for lesser reasons,' he pointed out.

'True,' admitted Georgiou. 'OK, we'll look into her. God knows, we've got few enough suspects in this case. So far it's her, the would-be student film-maker, and our ranting hooded friend on the website.'

TWENTY-ONE

The X-rays confirmed that Georgiou did indeed have two cracked ribs, as well as cuts and bruises, but nothing else was broken.

'Which is something to be grateful for,' said Georgiou.

The one note of concern expressed by the doctor was that of concussion, especially while driving.

'No problem, doctor,' said Tennyson. 'I'll drive him home.'

'I'm fine to drive,' insisted Georgiou. 'It was just a bang on the head.'

'One hard enough to render you unconscious,' said the doctor. 'The brain is a mysterious organ. Despite all our advances in science and medicine, there's still a lot we don't know about it. Sometimes apparent recovery can be temporary.'

'See?' said Tennyson. 'I'll drive you home.'

'But what about my car?'

Just then, Tennyson's mobile rang. He gave an apologetic look at the doctor's disapproving expression.

'Sorry,' he mumbled. 'I thought I'd switched it off.'

He headed for the main reception as he answered the

phone.

'Take my advice, let your colleague drive you home, and then rest. Is there anyone at home to take care of you?'

'I'll be fine,' Georgiou reassured the doctor.

Inwardly, he thought: no, there's no one to take care of me. Not any more, not since Susannah died.

'If you don't promise me to let yourself be driven home, and to rest once you get there, I may not allow you to leave,' said the doctor.

'You can't afford the beds,' countered Georgiou.

'I'll find one,' said the doctor.

Tennyson returned, once again giving an apologetic look at the doctor.

'Sorry about that,' he said again. Turning to Georgiou, he said: 'That was Seward. Billy Patterson's disappeared. They've got uniform calling on all his known pals, places where he hangs out. We'll find him, guv.'

'Good,' said Georgiou.

'And Seward says she'll follow us in your car.'

'What?'

'When I drive you home. You were worried about leaving your car where it is, so we'll go and pick it up. Then she'll follow us in it, and I'll drive us both back."

'It's not necessary,' said Georgiou.

'Yes it is,' said the doctor. 'On those grounds, I'll let you go.'

'And it's half past six,' said Tennyson. 'End of our shift. So, we're on our own time now. We can do what we want, and what we want to do is drive you home.'

Debby Seward drove along the coast road in Georgiou's Vauxhall. Ahead of her was Tennyson's car, a green VW beetle. There was no chance of her losing the tail; they were the only two cars on this stretch of road. And, even if she did lose them, this road only went to one place: Bowness on Solway. All the turnings off went left, inland. To her right was the sea. This journey didn't need a map or Satnav, it was one no one could get lost on.

Her hands tightened on the steering wheel in anger as she thought of Georgiou being beaten up, and so badly he'd ended up in hospital. When she got hold of this rat, Billy Patterson, she'd make him wish he'd never been born. She'd kick his balls through his head. Break his ribs, see how he liked that.

No, she wouldn't. If she did, she'd just be handing Georgiou's enemies more ammunition. That's what this had all been about. Nothing to do with the murders. A gang of juvenile thugs from the Raffles estate. This was to do with Ian Parks. Revenge for Georgiou being reinstated after that 'incident' with Parks. The Parks family and that rat, Councillor Maitland, would be looking for any signs of what they could label 'police violence' to use against Georgiou, and if she damaged Patterson, as all her feelings told her she wanted to do, then they'd use that as evidence that this was the way Georgiou encouraged his officers to behave. So, no. When she finally got hold of Patterson she'd find some other way to make him squirm. She didn't know how, yet, but she'd think of something. That little bastard was going to pay dearly for what he did to Georgiou.

She did her best to make her fingers relax on the

steering wheel. *His* steering wheel. Oh, if only she could hold his hand! When she'd heard about him being beaten unconscious, she wanted to run to the A&E and hold him, tell him how much he meant to her. God, that would have caused a stir! That would have set tongues wagging.

But say he hadn't responded? Say, instead of being flattered, he'd been shocked and rejected her. That would be the finish for her. She'd have to leave the force.

What did he feel about her? Anything? Or was she just a work colleague? After that one occasion when she'd held his hand sympathetically and told him she was there for him, there'd been nothing from him. But she was *sure* he had some kind of feeling for her. Sometimes when he looked at her, and he didn't realize that she was aware of him, she saw something in those deep brown eyes of his. Indecision, certainly, as if he wanted to say something to her, something personal. But he never did. Or was she just being over-imaginative?

If only she could get some time with him that wasn't about work. Like . . . now. This evening. Maybe tonight was the time to find out if there was something there, or if she was just wasting her time.

TWENTY-TWO

Seward pulled Georgiou's car to a halt behind Tennyson's. 'Right, thank you, my pair of nursemaids,' said Georgiou. 'I think I can make it to my front door from here.'

'I'm sorry, sir,' she found herself blurting out. 'I still don't think that's a good idea.'

Georgiou and Tennyson looked at her, puzzled.

'What isn't?' asked Georgiou.

'You see, there was a cousin of mine. Mark,' said Seward. She was gabbling now, but trying to sound coherent. 'He fell off a ladder and banged his head. Only a little knock. Everyone thought he was fine. The hospital sent him home, and that same evening he collapsed at home and died. Brain haemorrhage.'

'The hospital did an X-ray of my skull,' Georgiou pointed out.

'Yes, but that's just the bone,' countered Seward. 'My cousin Mark said he was fine, too. And he was. But then, three hours later, he was dead.'

'So what do you suggest?' demanded Georgiou. He looked at his watch. 'It's half past seven. You two stay and watch me until the magic hour of half past ten?'

Tennyson looked uncomfortable.

'I'm afraid I can't do that, boss,' he said. 'It's my turn to put the kids to bed.'

'I'm not asking you to!' Georgiou snapped irritably.

'I can,' said Seward.

The two men looked at her, both puzzled.

'I haven't got anyone to go home for,' said Seward hurriedly. 'And I'd never forgive myself if I went and you collapsed and died.'

'I'd phone 999,' said Georgiou.

'You wouldn't be able to if you collapsed suddenly,' insisted Seward.

'She's got a point,' said Tennyson.

Georgiou pointed to his car.

'And how will you get home?' he asked.

Maybe I won't, thought Seward. Maybe this is when things change. Aloud, she said: 'I'll drive home, and come back and pick you up in the morning.'

Georgiou shook his head doubtfully.

'It seems a lot of fuss over nothing,' he said.

'That's what my cousin Mark said,' defended Seward. 'And look what happened to him. The doctors said that if someone had been with him when he collapsed, he might have been saved.'

'It's worth considering, guv,' added Tennyson.

Georgiou gave a heavy sigh.

'OK,' he said. 'You seem determined, and I'm in no fit state to spend time arguing with you.' He turned to Tennyson. 'I'll see you in the morning, Mac. And, if I die in the meantime,

DS Seward will be able to let you know.'

'It's not something to joke about,' said Seward angrily.

Immediately, Georgiou gave her an apologetic look, remembering that she'd had a personal experience of such a tragedy with her cousin.

'I'm sorry, Debby,' he said. 'I didn't mean to be flippant.' He gestured at his front door. 'Let's go and get that kettle on. I'm dying for a coffee.'

While Debby Seward made them coffee, Georgiou went upstairs, showered, and then changed his blood-spattered clothes into something clean. Every movement he made caused him pain. Those thugs had done a good job on him.

He thought of Seward, downstairs. It was the first time he'd been alone with a woman in his house since Susannah died. At least, an attractive, available woman. If Seward was available, that was. There didn't seem to be anyone else in her life, otherwise she wouldn't have been able to just offer to stay and keep an eye on him.

He dismissed the thought. She was a colleague, his detective sergeant. Romantic liaisons between officers was frowned upon. Stokes would leap upon it if he even thought there was something going on between Georgiou and Seward. The chance to get rid of Georgiou for 'disciplinary reasons'. And maybe get rid of Seward, too. Not that there was any such thing going on.

But she was an attractive woman. A very attractive woman. And it had been a long time since Georgiou had held a woman like her in his arms. Felt her arms around him. Felt her lips touching his, his arms touching her body, her hands touching him . . .

Stop this! he told himself. We have to get out of this house, somewhere where there are other people around.

He limped downstairs, and found Seward sitting at the kitchen table with two cups of coffee.

'OK,' he said. 'Coffee's fine, but after the day I've had, what say we grab a meal and a drink at the pub. I don't fancy cooking tonight, and I wouldn't dream of asking you to negotiate my oven. And I'm not even sure what I've got in the cupboard. Plus, it's getting late.'

Seward looked at him, taken aback by this list of reasons why they shouldn't eat here, even though it was all said with a friendly smile.

'Yes,' she said. 'Sounds a good idea, sir.'

'Can we drop the "sir" business while we're in the pub?' he asked.

She hesitated.

'What should I call you?'

I don't know, Georgiou realized. The members of his team always called him sir, or guv, or chief. He didn't want to set a precedent, where suddenly his junior officers were on first-name terms with him, no matter what directives came down from head office about 'adopting an informal team-led approach'.

'Maybe don't call me anything,' he suggested. 'Anyway, we may not have much chance to talk tonight, once it's nine o'clock. I've just realized that tonight is quiz night at the pub. Once the questions start, there's a very serious atmosphere there. No idle chatter.' He gave her a grin. 'We can form a team, if you like. It might be fun. A break from running around after serial killers. Getting beaten up.'

'Just the two of us?' asked Seward, frowning. 'Is two a team?'

'There might be someone spare, there usually is,' said Georgiou. 'So, what do you say?'

TWENTY-THREE

The Kings Arms was half full when Georgiou and Seward entered. Georgiou led the way to a table where a bearded man was sitting alone with a nearly empty pint glass.

'Hi, Denis,' said Georgiou.

Denis peered at Georgiou.

'My God, someone gave you a going over, and no mistake!' he said. 'What happened?'

'I'll tell you later,' said Georgiou. He gestured at the two empty chairs. 'Are these seats taken?'

'They will be once you sit down,' said Denis.

'Good,' said Georgiou, and gestured for Seward to sit. 'This is Debby Seward, a colleague of mine. Debby, this is Denis Irving. Farmer, local historian, and a fount of all knowledge about Carlisle United football club.'

'Pleased to meet you,' said Seward, shaking hands.

'So, plain clothes or just out of uniform?' asked Denis.

'Debby's a detective sergeant,' said Georgiou. 'What are you drinking?'

'Jennings,' said Denis. 'Thanks.'

'Debby?'

'A tonic water with ice and lemon.'

'Driving?' asked Denis.

Seward nodded.

'I'll order us something to eat while I'm at the bar,' said Georgiou. 'What do you fancy?'

'What's good?' asked Seward.

'Everything,' said Denis. 'Jenny's a really good cook.'

'I'll get you a menu,' said Georgiou.

He headed for the bar, while Denis studied Seward.

'This is very rare, Andy bringing one of his colleagues in here,' he said. 'In fact, you're the first, as far as I can recall.'

'Yes, well, he needed a driver tonight.'

'Oh? Something to do with those bruises and the cut lip?'

'Er. . . .' Seward hesitated, wondering if Georgiou would like her talking about what had happened to him. She decided not, so instead she just smiled.

Georgiou returned and handed her a menu.

'Drinks are on their way,' he said.

Seward gave Georgiou a desperate look.

'I didn't say anything,' she said.

'No need,' said Georgiou, grinning. 'Denis is one of the brightest people I know. He'll have worked it all out. He should have been a detective.'

'I prefer cows,' said Denis. 'You know where you are with cows. So, what happened? Or is it an official secret?'

'I ran into some people who didn't like me,' said Georgiou. 'They beat me up.' He gestured at the menu in Seward's hand. 'So, what do you fancy?' he asked.

Seward scanned the menu, then said: 'The chicken pie.'

'Good choice,' said Denis approvingly. 'Handmade. Like I say, Jenny is a good cook.'

Georgiou returned to the bar to place their order, then came back with three drinks held in his hands: a pint each for himself and Denis, and a tonic water for Seward. By now the pub had begun to fill up as more people filtered in through the door.

'Quiz night,' said Denis to Seward. 'Fifteen minutes more and this place'll be packed.'

'Yes, so . . .' Seward was about to say 'Andy', but stopped herself. Instead, she finished with 'So I hear'.

'So, what's your speciality?' asked Denis.

'Speciality?' queried Seward.

'For the quiz. I assume we're a team,' he said, looking at Georgiou.

'We are,' agreed Georgiou, sipping at his pint.

'Films,' said Seward.

'Right, that's you with films, me with local history and agriculture, Andy here with pop music . . .'

'Pop music?' echoed Seward, surprised.

'The eighties are his speciality,' said Denis. 'That and football. Except for Carlisle United, of course, that's my area.'

'I do follow Carlisle,' protested Georgiou. 'I always check their results.'

'Yes, but you haven't been following them as long as I have,' pointed out Denis. 'You don't know all the names of all the old players.'

'No,' admitted Georgiou. 'But I can name all the Arsenal Invincibles team of the 2003-2004 season.'

'Arsenal!' snorted Denis derisively. 'They didn't even have any English players! All French and African!'

'That's where you're wrong!' countered Georgiou. 'Ashley Cole. Sol Campbell. Martin Keown. Ray Parlour . . .'

Seward sat and watched him, feeling both slightly bewildered and also amused. She'd never seen Georgiou like this before: relaxed, despite his injuries, talking about something other than the job. There was an easiness to him in here, which the team didn't see on a day-to-day basis. At work, Georgiou was all business, intense, determined, driven.

She sipped at her tonic water. Maybe if I had a glass of wine next, she thought. Enough for him to say that I shouldn't really drive, and suggest I could stay the night in his spare room. Or in the living room on his settee. Or, maybe . . .

Stop thinking like this, she told herself sharply. You'll drive yourself mad. Or mess things up.

Denis pointed at her glass. She was aware that he and Georgiou had nearly finished their beers.

'Same again?' he asked.

'I'll get these,' she said, and hurried quickly to the bar.

The landlord, a friendly-looking man with glasses and a moustache, smiled at her.

'What can I get you?' he asked.

'Two pints of Jennings,' she said. 'And a glass of . . . of tonic water.'

She carried the drinks back to the table.

'Still on tonic water?' asked Denis.

'Yes,' she said.

'A law-abiding copper,' said Denis, nodding approvingly.

'That's good to know.'

There's still a chance, Seward told herself. When we finish here, he still might decide it's too late for me to drive home, and suggest I stay rather than have to come all the way back in the morning.

'Still, if you're driving back home tonight, and I'm guessing you're in his car, how's Andy getting to work tomorrow?' asked Denis.

'She's coming to pick me up in the morning,' said Georgiou.

'Where from?'

'Carlisle,' said Seward.

'That's ridiculous!' snorted Denis. 'Going back all that way tonight, and then coming back in a few hours.' He shook his head. 'Makes no sense.'

No, it doesn't, thought Seward, but she hoped that Denis hadn't raised the issue too soon. She'd hoped that Georgiou might say the same thing, but later.

'I'll drop Andy off in Carlisle tomorrow,' said Denis. 'I've got to go in anyway and go to the Mart.'

'Would you?' asked Georgiou.

No! Seward felt herself wanting to shout out. No! This is my chance!

'No problem,' said Denis cheerfully. He smiled at Seward. 'It'll save you making an unnecessary trip.'

'That's very decent of you, Denis,' said Georgiou. He smiled at Seward, and as she looked at his battered face, the cuts and bruises, and those twinkling eyes of his, Seward's heart melted. 'He's a good bloke, is Denis.'

Yes, thought Seward, but inside she felt numb, as if

everything she'd hoped for had just been snatched away.

At 10.30, Seward, Georgiou and Denis left the pub. It had been an unusual evening. They hadn't won the quiz, although they'd come close. There had only been two questions about films, both of which Seward had got right. The trouble was, because they'd been easy questions, nearly everyone else had got them. The meal had been excellent, as good as Denis had said it would be. And once Denis had made that offer to run Georgiou in to Carlisle the next day, an offer that Georgiou had so eagerly snatched up, Seward had stuck to non-alcoholic drinks for the whole evening. A pity, she thought. It would have been great to unwind with a glass or three of wine. And afterwards, go back to Georgiou's house with him.

Denis waved them goodbye and walked off down the street, and Georgiou and Seward walked to where his car was parked.

'You sure you're going to be all right driving back?' he asked.

What do I answer? she wondered. Do I say, 'No, I'm feeling really tired,' and hope he suggests I crash out at his place? But then what? A sleepless night in his spare bed, lying there, hoping.

'I'll be fine,' she said. 'How do you feel?'

'No concussion.' He smiled. 'I'm good.' He hesitated, and for a brief moment Seward thought he was going to ask her in. But then she was sure he gave a brief sigh before he said: 'I'll see you in the morning.'

'Yes,' she said, even though she wanted to throw herself

at him, throw her arms around him, kiss him. 'Tomorrow.'

With that she walked to Georgiou's car, unlocked it, got in, started the engine, and drove away.

Georgiou stood watching the red tail lights of his car as it disappeared. Then he opened his front door, and into went his house. He didn't see the slight, slim figure standing in the shadows by the corner of the pub, watching him.

TWENTY-FOUR

The next morning, Denis picked Georgiou up and drove him to Carlisle. Being a farmer, used to getting up early to arrange milking, Denis liked to get an early start, before the 'commuter traffic', as he called it, clogged up the roads. As a result, Georgiou was walking in to the police HQ at quarter past eight.

'Morning, Inspector!' the desk sergeant, Andy Graham, greeted him. 'Feeling all right?'

'Better than I was yesterday,' replied Georgiou. 'Anyone in?'

'DS Conway,' said Graham.

Georgiou frowned. This was early for Conway.

'Where is he?' he asked.

'In the briefing room.'

'Thanks,' said Georgiou, and made his way there. If Conway was in this early, it could mean that there'd been a development. On which case? he wondered. The head-hunting serial killer, or the search for Billy Patterson?

He pushed open the glass door to the briefing room, and immediately registered the look of concern on Conway's face.

'What's up?' he asked. 'Did you get that CCTV footage from Tait Street?'

Conway shook his head.

'There was no film in the camera,' he said sourly.

'What?' said Georgiou.

'Cuts to the council budget,' said Conway. 'At least, that's the official explanation. They keep the cameras there as a deterrent, but they can't afford to put film in. Or disks, or whatever it is they use.'

'Incredible!' said Georgiou, shaking his head in disbelief.

'Actually, that's not the problem,' said Conway awkwardly.

'It sounds like one to me!' growled Georgiou. 'We could have got a vehicle! A number plate!'

'It's Richard Little,' said Conway, sounding and looking very uncomfortable.

Georgiou frowned. 'What is?' he asked.

'The problem,' said Conway, adding, 'He's missing.'

'Missing?'

Conway nodded.

'I called at his house again this morning, and he wasn't there. Vera said he hadn't been home all night. She was worried, but she tried not to show it.'

What was it Dr Kirtle had said? We're looking for someone neat and tidy. Fastidious. Georgiou's own words flashed through his mind again: We're looking for someone like Little.

No, it was madness. But Conway was still looking at him, awkwardly, and Georgiou could tell Conway was thinking the same thing: the unthinkable.

'I know it sounds mad, but you don't think that Richard might be. . .?' Conway's voice trailed off.

'Our killer?' said Georgiou. Trying to bring some sanity back to the situation, he said, 'It's bit of a leap. He's missing. Could be any number of reasons.'

'Like what?' asked Conway. 'Look how careful this killer's been not to leave clues. A copper's perfect for that. Any copper would know what we'd be looking for, and make sure they didn't leave traces.'

Georgiou thought it over.

'You spend more time with him than anyone else,' he said. 'What do you think?'

'To be honest, he's been acting a bit strange of late,' said Conway. 'I don't know what to think.' Then he added: 'Then there was that business with the Reivers.'

'Which turned out to be a dead end,' said Georgiou.

'Yes, but maybe that wasn't the point,' said Conway. 'He'd said about it to me earlier, and I'd told him it was a dead end and to forget it, but he brought it up anyway. And remember what he said: "It's *my* name. Little."'

'He was talking about Reiver names.'

'That's what I thought, but say he wasn't. Say he was trying to tell us something. Like . . . "It's me".'

Georgiou mulled it over. It was too simple. But then, often things were simple.

'I think we'd better go and have a chat with Vera Little,' said Georgiou.

He walked to his desk and checked his e-mails.

'Ah-ha!' he said. 'We have a result!'

'On what?' asked Conway.

'On our hooded ranting friend,' said Georgiou. He moved to one side so that Conway could read through the e-mail from GCHQ. It was very basic: 'Re website threat: 14-year old arrested in Truro, Cornwall. No known terrorist connections. No accomplices. Footage filmed by webcam in culprit's bedroom. Detailed information follows.'

'So, as we suspected, some teenage loner in his bedroom declaring war on society from a webcam in his bedroom,' sighed Georgiou.

The sound of the door opening made them both turn. Kirsty Taggart had just come in, and she looked very pleased with herself.

'I thought you'd be interested to know that we've got your friend Patterson downstairs.'

'Patterson?' queried Georgiou, momentarily thrown. His mind was still racing on the news about Richard Little.

'The antichrist,' said Taggart, grinning. 'The thug who attacked you. Debby and I decided to make an early start, thinking we'd catch him at one of the addresses while he was still half asleep. It worked. We found him at his own place.'

'Well done,' said Georgiou. 'Where is he?'

'We've put him in one of the interview rooms,' said Taggart. 'Debby's with him.' She grinned again. 'Mind, he protests his innocence. Says he hasn't done anything.'

'They all say that,' snorted Conway derisively. Then, awkwardly, to Georgiou, he said: 'What do you want me to do about . . .' He let the rest of the sentence hang.

'Fill in the rest of the team as they come in,' said Georgiou. 'Start with Kirsty here. Let them know

155

everything you know. Then we'll talk about it after I've talked to our young friend.' Turning to Taggart, he asked: 'Did you say that Seward's with him?'

Taggart nodded.

'Right,' said Georgiou. 'I'll let her interview him. Thugs hate having a woman question them. Makes them feel . . . small.'

Georgiou opened the door of the interview room. Seward was sitting at one side of a table. Across from her was a young man with a sallow complexion, riddled with acne. He had an almost shaven head and rings through his ears and his nose. Next to him sat a smartly dressed woman who Georgiou recognized as one of the regular duty solicitors, Janine Evans. So Patterson didn't have his own brief. A uniformed police officer stood at one side, watching.

Evans and Seward both looked at Georgiou as he stood in the doorway. Billy Patterson kept his head studiously away from Georgiou.

'Ms Evans.' Georgiou nodded politely towards the solicitor, and she nodded back. Then he turned to Seward. 'Sergeant, can we have a brief word, please?'

With a nod at the uniformed officer, Seward got up and followed Georgiou out into the corridor. Georgiou pulled the door shut, then said: 'Thanks for last night.'

'I didn't do anything,' said Seward. 'Just ran you home.'

'You did a lot more than that,' said Georgiou quietly. He wanted to say more, much more, tell her how much he'd wanted her to stay, but this wasn't the time or the place for it. Instead, he said: 'Well done on getting hold of Patterson.'

'It wasn't that difficult,' she said. 'He was at home, in bed. Kirsty and I obviously called on him earlier than he expected. Despite the fact that he must have known we were looking for him, with uniforms knocking on the doors of all his friends, asking for him. I think he's got the brain cells of an onion.'

'Lucky he has, otherwise our success rate wouldn't be half as good as it is.' commented Georgiou. 'Anyway, you do the interview.'

Seward threw him a questioning look.

'It's your collar,' said Georgiou. 'I'll just be there, in the background, listening and watching. Let's make him sweat.'

'OK.' Seward nodded.

They went back into the room, and Seward took her chair opposite Billy Patterson. Georgiou remained standing, keeping his distance, but watching Patterson and Evans. Georgiou could tell that Seward handling the interview while he just observed had unsettled Patterson, even though he tried to hide it beneath an air of sullen bravado.

Seward switched on the tape recorder.

'Interview began at 08.30 hours,' she said. 'Present: Detective Sergeant Seward, Detective Inspector Georgiou, William Patterson, Ms Janine Evans representing Mr Patterson.' Addressing Patterson directly, she said: 'Please state your full name and address.'

The youth shot a glance at the solicitor beside him, as if hoping she would tell him he didn't need to do this, but she nodded for him to give the information. Reluctantly, sullenly, he mumbled something.

'Would you make your reply louder, please, for the

purposes of the tape,' said Seward.

Patterson was obviously discomforted by this, like a naughty boy in class who is being told off by his teacher, but when a further look for help towards his solicitor received nothing but another nod, he spoke again, louder this time, his voice strained and awkward.

'William Patterson. 15 Mardale Road, Carlisle.'

Seward looked down at a sheet of paper in front of her, then said: 'And that is your full name?'

'Yeah.' Patterson scowled.

'Then you are not also known as William *George* Patterson?' asked Seward.

A frown crossed Patterson's face.

'Well, yeah . . .' he said. 'But I don't use that bit.'

Seward didn't respond, but looked at him unsmilingly and said firmly: 'Please state your *full* name.'

Patterson shifted uncomfortably, then said: 'William George Patterson.'

Good, thought Georgiou. Start with a small victory. Chip away at that smug, arrogant exterior. Wear him down.

'Where were you at half past four yesterday afternoon?' asked Seward.

'One moment . . .' It was Janine Evans, speaking for the first time. 'Surely my client needs to be told *why* he is being interviewed before asking him specific details?'

At this Patterson gave a smirk. Georgiou could imagine him thinking, That's it! You tell 'em!

Seward carried on looking directly into Patterson's face as she said: 'Because of the serious nature of the case we are investigating, that information will have to come later.'

'But surely . . .' began Evans.

Seward didn't let her speak.

'As I said, this is a very serious case with associated investigations coinciding. Consequently we need to decide whether your client will form part of our ongoing investigation, and we need to determine that from his answers.'

The rush of hard words and the very firm way in which Seward delivered this left Patterson looking bewildered. Aloud, and defiantly, he said: 'I didn't beat him up.'

Calmly, Seward said: 'For the purposes of the tape, let it be known that the interviewee's statement was not prompted by any question.'

Then she looked across the table directly into Patterson's eyes.

'Tell us about Tamara Armstrong,' said Seward.

At this, Patterson looked absolutely bewildered. Georgiou could tell that Evans was also puzzled at this line of questioning, and she opened her mouth to say something, but Seward held up a hand to silence her.

'I must ask you again for your connection to, or knowledge of, Tamara Armstrong.'

'I don't know what you're talking about!' said Patterson, obviously completely baffled. Georgiou could imagine the turmoil in Patterson's brain; a brain that wouldn't be the brightest at the best of times. Here he was, being battered by official, hard-sounding jargon, police-speak, about something he hadn't anticipated. He would have had his alibi already cooked up for the time when Georgiou was being beaten up; the times and events rehearsed and held like rote in his mind, but the questions had taken a turn he hadn't expected.

'What about Mr Han Sun?' asked Seward.

Patterson just gaped at her, then turned to his solicitor, who said: 'Sergeant, I was under the impression that my client was being questioned about an assault . . .'

Seward didn't let her finish.

'We are currently investigating the murders of Tamara Armstrong and Han Sun,' said Seward. 'We have reason to believe the assault on Inspector Georgiou is connected with both these murders . . .'

'Oh no you don't!' said the youth, getting to his feet, agitated.

The uniformed officer made a move to step forward and grab Patterson, but Georgiou waved for him to stay where he was.

'Please sit down,' said Seward crisply.

When Patterson didn't sit, just began pacing, Seward said: 'For the purposes of the tape, the suspect left his chair and refused to sit down.'

For her part, Evans was doing her best to recover her composure.

The youth stood, torn apart by what was happening to him, then he sat down and looked at Seward feverishly across the table. All smug defiance was gone from him now.

'This is nothing to do with any murder,' he said. 'Parksy said we were just teaching him a lesson.'

'Parksy?'

'Ian Parks.'

'Is this the same Ian Parks that Inspector Georgiou

arrested for attempted theft?' asked Seward.

The youth nodded.

'My client . . .' began Evans, desperate to stop her client from incriminating himself further, but Patterson was having none of it. He'd thought he was being pulled in for attacking a copper. Now he saw himself in the frame for two murders, and that was a different ballgame. He was going to get himself off that particular hook, whatever it took.

'Parksy said we shouldn't have these people coming into our country and telling us what to do, and beating us up like they owned the place.'

'Which people?' asked Seward.

'Foreigners,' said Patterson. Pointing at Georgiou he said, 'People like him.'

'And the names of the other people involved in the attack on Inspector Georgiou?' asked Seward.

The youth hesitated, then turned towards Evans appealingly, but his solicitor had already mentally washed her hands of him. He'd already made a confession of his own guilt, and in her presence, and on tape. He could only make his own situation worse by refusing to name his accomplices. Seward waited, eyes fixed firmly on Patterson, her gaze drilling into his skull.

'They're my mates,' he begged, helplessly.

It cut no ice with Seward, or anyone else in that room. Patterson looked around, as if there was some salvation for him, but all he got back was hard looks and blank, unfriendly walls. He was lost, and he knew it. Finally, the youth dropped his head and mumbled something.

'Speak up, please,' said Seward. 'For the tape.'

The youth lifted his head.

'Ian Parks. Denny Goff. Steve Andrews.'

Seward pushed a pad and pen across to Patterson.

'Write down their addresses, please,' she said.

TWENTY-FIVE

Georgiou watched while Seward took down Patterson's confession and got him to sign it in front of his solicitor, before she despatched the frightened youth to the holding cells in the presence of a constable.

'Well done,' he said. 'That was a great interview. You handled him perfectly.'

Seward held up the handwritten list of addresses that Patterson had given her.

'Next, I'll send uniform round to these places and bring these three in,' she said. 'Or I might go myself, just to give myself the pleasure of seeing the looks on their faces when I tell them their good pal, Billy Patterson, has shopped them.'

Georgiou shook his head. 'Right now, I've got some new information for the team, and you need to hear it.'

'Oh?'

'Richard Little's gone missing.'

Seward stared at him.

'What do you mean, missing?' she asked.

'I'll tell you as we head for the briefing room,' said Georgiou.

By the time the two of them reached their destination, Georgiou had filled the stunned Seward in on what Conway had told him about Little, and their suspicions. As they entered the briefing room, Georgiou could see from the shocked expression on the faces of Tennyson and Taggart that they were also having difficulty coming to terms with the possibility that Richard Little was their murderer.

'But . . . he's one of us!' said Taggart, shaking her head.

'He's also missing,' said Georgiou. 'And, as Conway pointed out to me earlier, there's no one like a copper for knowing how to avoid getting caught.'

'He wouldn't be the first,' added Conway sombrely.

'But why?' asked Taggart. 'Why would he kill those people?'

'Why would anyone?' said Tennyson, and he gave a heavy sigh. 'This is unbelievable!'

'Whether we like it or not, we have to accept that Richard Little is a suspect,' said Georgiou. 'We need to check his movements on the nights of the murders. I'll do that. I'll go and see his wife, Vera, see what she can tell me.'

'Someone ought to go with you, guv,' said Tennyson. 'Remember what happened the last time you went out on your own.'

'Yes, thank you for that, Sergeant,' grunted Georgiou. 'But I think I should be safe from attack from Vera Little.'

'Say Richard hasn't disappeared at all,' put in Seward. 'Say he's hiding in the house and his wife's protecting him. If he hears you asking questions he might get rough.'

Georgiou sighed wearily.

'OK,' he said. 'Looks like you're determined to nursemaid

me. Conway, you come with me. You know Vera Little better than any of us. You might be able to work out if she's covering for him. Also, let's put out an alert for him. No need to state why we're looking for him, just a missing persons report, Detective Constable Richard Little. Full description to all forces, and ports and airports. After all, he could be anywhere, or trying to get away. Mac, will you deal with that?'

Tennyson nodded as he made a note on his pad.

Turning to Seward and Taggart, Georgiou asked: 'By the way, I meant to ask you before I got clattered the other day: how did you two get on with the film man? Drake?'

Seward's face wrinkled in disgust, and Taggart laughed.

'He's a health hazard,' said Taggart. 'If we're looking for someone who's fastidious and neat and obsessively clean, then Drake is not our man.'

'But the film he's making is interesting,' said Seward. 'I read the script. It's about pagan sacrifice.'

'Shades of Diane Moody,' commented Tennyson.

'What sort of sacrifice?' asked Georgiou.

'Ripping a body open and reading the entrails,' said Seward. 'After the victim's been ritually killed by crows.'

'Any beheading in it?'

'Only after the body's been ripped open,' said Seward.

'Anything about Hadrian's Wall?' asked Tennyson, remembering his conversation with Diane Moody.

'No,' said Seward. 'Just Ancient Britons. But there's a nasty feel to it. Gratuitous violence, just to shock.'

'It's definitely worth a closer look,' said Georgiou. 'This Drake character may not be the one we're looking for, but get a list of everyone involved in the film. Wardrobe, camera, extras, lighting, everyone. And start digging, looking for a connection with the murder victims.'

'They start shooting the film tomorrow at Castlerigg Stone Circle,' said Seward. 'The whole crew will be there all in one place.'

'Great.' Georgiou nodded. 'A perfect opportunity.' Turning to Tennyson, Georgiou said: 'Mac, after you've put out the alert for Richard Little, I want you to dig into these attacks by Ian Parks a bit more.'

'Any particular direction?' asked Tennyson.

Georgiou nodded.

'I've checked the names of the women he attacked.' He pulled a piece of paper from his pocket and read out: 'Mrs de Laglio, Mrs Izmir, Mrs Woycek.'

'Italian, Turkish and Polish,' murmured Taggart.

'Exactly,' said Georgiou.

'No, they're not,' said Tennyson. 'I've talked to them all. They're all English.'

'Second or third generation, maybe. But with a foreign name,' said Georgiou. 'Just like me.'

'You think these are racist attacks?' asked Seward.

'Yes,' said Georgiou. 'There's no doubt these women were chosen because they were old and couldn't defend themselves, and the motive was money . . . but there's a racist element here. Like the attitude of Patterson when he was interviewed.'

A thought struck Georgiou.

'What political party does Maitland represent?'

Tennyson shook his head. 'None,' he said. 'Independent.'

'Which covers an awful lot of possibilities. Run some checks on Maitland and the Parks family. Cross-check against any right-wing organizations. National Front, BNP, Combat 18, Spear of Destiny, that sort of thing.'

Tennyson nodded.

'Will do,' he said. 'How much time do you want me to give it?'

Georgiou thought about it. He'd love to nail Maitland as a racist, but right now the murder investigation and the search for Richard Little had to take priority.

'At this moment, no time at all,' he said regretfully. 'Let's forget it until after we've nailed our killer and found Richard.'

Tennyson nodded.

'OK, guv,' he said.

'Right,' said Georgiou, addressing the whole team. 'Let's all go and do some investigating.'

TWENTY-SIX

Georgiou was walking with Conway towards Conway's car, when his mobile rang. He checked the name and number on the display screen and saw it was Dr Kirtle, the pathologist.

'Georgiou,' he said.

'I've got the results of the tests on the body of Han Sun,' said Dr Kirtle. 'There's something different from the previous two murders.'

'Oh?'

'Traces of a tranquilizer,' said Dr Kirtle.

'What sort of tranquilizer?' asked Georgiou.

'Do you want the full chemical name, or just where it's normally used?' asked Kirtle.

'The easy-to-understand one,' said Georgiou.

'It's the sort used by vets to knock out animals,' said Dr Kirtle. 'I'll be e-mailing my full report over to you shortly, but I thought you'd want to know as soon as possible.'

'Yes, I do,' said Georgiou. 'Thanks.'

He hung up and told Conway what Dr Kirtle had just told him.

'A vet connection?' hazarded Conway.

'Maybe,' said Georgiou. 'We'll start checking vets and their supplies later.'

His mobile rang again.

'We'll never get to Vera's at this rate,' he grunted.

This time the number on the screen was that of Dan Murphy, the news editor of the *Cumberland News*. Georgiou grinned to himself; he could guess what this was about. But he liked Dan, so he wasn't going to just ignore him.

'Dan,' he greeted him. 'Let me guess: Jenny McAndrew's been on to you complaining that I won't talk to her.'

Georgiou heard Murphy chuckle, and pictured him sitting in his office at the *Cumberland News*, leaning back in his chair, a polystyrene cup of strong black coffee on his desk, most of which would remain undrunk.

'You're into mind-reading now, are you, Andreas?' said Murphy.

'With a mind like Jenny McAndrew's, that's easy to read,' said Georgiou.

'I hear you got beaten up,' said Murphy.

'You pick up news fast,' said Georgiou.

'It is my job,' Murphy reminded him. 'Look, Andreas, you and I have always got on, haven't we? I've treated what you've told me in confidence when it's been needed, and put out stuff when you needed it to flush out a crook or two.'

'True,' agreed Georgiou. 'It's a pity your colleague Jenny McAndrew doesn't follow the same rules.'

'The *News and Star* doesn't come under the same remit—' began Murphy, but Georgiou cut him off with a rueful laugh.

'Don't give me that, Dan. The *News and Star* and the

Cumberland News are two peas in the same pod. One's weekly, one's daily. One's broadsheet size, one's tabloid size, but everything in them comes out of the same office.'

'OK, OK,' Murphy agreed, but reluctantly. 'Look, McAndrew's new. And maybe she got off on the wrong foot . . .'

'Maybe?' said Georgiou. 'Did you read her piece she did on me?'

'Yes, and if I'd been in the office on that day I'd have spiked it,' said Murphy. 'The trouble was I was away when it came in and there was all hell over Tamara Armstrong being murdered, so no one at the top was checking the smaller stuff.'

'So a whole half a page allegation of my beating up some poor innocent kid is smaller stuff, is it?' said Georgiou.

'You know what I mean,' said Murphy. 'The trouble is Jenny wants to make a name for herself so she can get on one of the big tabloids down south, and she wants to do it fast.'

'As far as I'm concerned the sooner she moves down south and stops bothering me, the better,' said Georgiou.

'Look, Andreas, whether you like it or not, we can be a help to you on this case. We can get stuff out to the general public.'

'True,' acknowledged Georgiou.

'So, why don't we get together? You and me and McAndrew? Come on, Andreas, this is the biggest story that's happened here for years . . .'

'So I'm told,' said Georgiou. 'The superintendent says that even the American media have been on to him.'

'And you want to cut out the locals, just because this kid has got your back up?'

'No, because this "kid", as you call her, distorted what I said to her. So who's to say she won't do the same again but with worse consequences. We're dealing with a murderer. I don't want her distorting things because she's so eager to make a name for herself that someone else gets murdered because of it.'

He heard Murphy sigh.

'OK, you and me. I'll leave her out of it. What do you say?'

Georgiou thought it over.

'Superintendent Stokes has ordered me not to talk to the press. All press enquiries have to go through him, or press liaison.'

'Oh, come on, Andreas! Stokes is about as useful as tits on a bicycle! We can help you, and you know it.'

'OK,' said Georgiou. 'But it'll all have to be off the record, and you'll need to reconfirm it with Stokes.'

'That suits me,' said Murphy. 'Shall I drop in to the office?'

'Not a good idea,' said Georgiou. 'Anyway, I've got to go and see someone. I'll call you when I've finished.'

'Don't leave it too long,' urged Murphy. 'This is a big story.'

'Really?' said Georgiou. 'I hadn't realized.'

Vera Little had always struck Georgiou as like a tiny house mouse in a Beatrix Potter book. Small and very neat, almost starched. Tidy to the point of obsession. Perpetually frowning as if looking for something wrong for her to

171

correct. Richard Little had struck Georgiou as the same. Richard and Vera Little, a pair of tiny, neat and obsessive book-ends. Now, in her fastidiously clean living room, Vera Little seemed to be doing her best to cling on to her proper and best behaviour, but Georgiou could see that tears were just a word away.

She sat on the edge of the settee, twisting a handkerchief in her hand. Now and then she dabbed at her eyes with it. Georgiou sat in an armchair and listened, his face showing his concern. Conway sat in the other armchair, looking very awkward. This was his partner they were talking about.

'I just don't know where he is or what could have happened to him,' said Vera, and once more she dabbed at her eyes. 'He's never done this kind of thing before. Never gone without saying a word. I wondered if it was something to do with this special operation he's been on lately.'

'Special operation?' queried Georgiou, doing his best to keep the surprise out of his voice.

Vera nodded.

'He's been on some kind of surveillance which means he had to be out a lot at night. All night. I know you're not allowed to tell me what it is, but I know he hasn't been happy about it.'

Oh God, no, thought Georgiou. Another piece in the jigsaw nailing Richard Little.

'I said to him he ought to ask you to be let off, but he's always been so conscientious. Always done his duty. You know that, Inspector.'

'Indeed I do.' Georgiou nodded sympathetically. 'When did you first notice this . . . night duty . . . getting him down?'

'Just before he started on it. About a month ago. It even seemed to hang over him when he wasn't on nights. I could tell he was worried, but . . .' She dabbed at her eyes again, then continued: 'I asked him what it was that was troubling him, but he wouldn't talk about it. And then, when these murders started, I knew it must be about them.'

A month ago, thought Georgiou. About the time that Michelle Nixon was murdered.

'Has he said anything lately about having any . . . personal problems?' asked Georgiou.

'What sort of personal problems?' asked Vera, and immediately there was a defensive tone to her voice.

Georgiou gave her a sympathetic smile and shrugged helplessly.

'I've no idea,' he said. 'To be honest, Vera, we're clutching at straws here. As you say, this is so completely unlike Richard. All we know is that he seems to have disappeared.'

Vera's face crumpled slightly and she dabbed at her eyes with the handkerchief again.

'You don't think . . .' she began in a voice that was barely above a frightened whisper '. . . you don't think this . . . murderer might have caught him? Killed him?'

Georgiou shook his head.

'I'm convinced that hasn't happened,' he said, with as much assurance as he could. 'This killer has made sure that the victims are found very quickly. No, I think for some reason we don't know about, Richard has decided to . . . slip away for a while.' A thought struck him. 'Has Richard been seeing his doctor lately? Is he on any form of medication?'

Vera shook her head. 'No,' she said. 'I think it's the stress of the job he's been doing. Working too hard. Days and nights.'

'You may be right,' agreed Georgiou. He knew he couldn't leave it like this. With so many questions needing answers, urgent answers, he had to tell Vera the truth.

'Vera, these night duties he's been doing . . .'

'Yes,' asked Vera.

'Did he tell you they were official?'

Vera looked at him, puzzled.

'Yes, of course,' she said. 'Why? Wasn't he supposed to tell me? He didn't say what he was actually doing. He was always very conscientious about not breaking a confidence.'

'I'm sure,' said Georgiou. 'The thing is, Vera, to the best of my knowledge, Richard wasn't on any official night surveillance duties. Not on police business.'

There was an awkward silence. Vera looked at him, and now the puzzled look on her face was one of complete confusion.

'What are you saying?' she asked, bewildered.

'I'm saying that whatever Richard was doing out at nights, to the best of my knowledge it wasn't on official police business.'

'But it must have been!' she burst out. 'He said it was!'

'If it was, I think I might have known about it,' said Georgiou gently. 'I certainly hadn't given him any instruction about working a night operation.'

'Then . . . then it must have been someone else!' said Vera desperately. 'He must have been working for someone else.'

'If so, no one's said anything to me about it,' said Georgiou. He looked across at Conway. 'Conway?'

Conway shook his head.

'Sorry, Vera,' he said uncomfortably.

'Then . . . what's he been doing all this time when he's been out?' she demanded. Angrily, she turned on Conway. 'Is there some other woman?'

'Not that I know of,' said Conway. 'He's never mentioned anyone to me but you.'

'But . . . this is madness!' spluttered Vera. 'This isn't like Richard!'

'I know,' said Georgiou. 'That's why we've got to find him, find out what's been going on. Vera, can you remember the dates when he was out at night on this . . . operation?'

'Why?' she demanded.

'It might give us a clue to what was going on. Which might help to lead us to him.'

She sat there, rigid now on the settee, the handkerchief crumpled tightly in her hand. Georgiou could almost see her mind racing, trying to cope with this sudden shocking news.

'I . . . I don't know,' she said.

'If you can, it will help us enormously. Help us find Richard for you. If you can search your mind, draw up a list of dates when you know he was out . . .'

'I don't see how that can help,' she said.

'Trust me, it will,' said Georgiou. 'At least it will give us somewhere to start looking. We can ask around, see if those dates mean anything to anyone at the station. After all, it could have been a secret operation that we didn't know about, but someone must.'

'Yes,' said Vera, grateful that some reason was forming to explain why Richard had stayed out so many nights. Any reason. Any excuse.

'If you could make out the list as soon as you can and phone us when it's ready,' said Georgiou. 'Iain will come over and pick it up.'

Vera nodded.

'This isn't like Richard,' she said, her voice urgent, insistent.

'I know,' agreed Georgiou. 'Don't worry, Vera, we'll find him.'

Georgiou and Conway waited until they were in the car before they spoke.

'Well, sir,' said Conway. 'This night stuff seems to clinch it, doesn't it? Looks like Richard's our man.'

'Maybe,' said Georgiou. 'But let's wait until we see what dates Vera comes up with. See if they match the killings.'

'She'll fix them,' said Conway. 'She knows what we're thinking. She'll make sure the dates don't match. She's no fool, is Vera.'

TWENTY-SEVEN

As soon as Georgiou and Conway got back to the station, Georgiou headed up the stairs to Stokes's office, but found the superintendent was out.

'He had to go to a lunch,' Stokes's secretary, a smart young woman called Deirdre Fisher, told him. Georgiou liked Fisher, knew her to be efficient and calm under pressure, the very opposite of Stokes. Georgiou wondered how she tolerated working for someone as insecure and unstable as Stokes.

Georgiou looked at his watch. It was three o'clock.

'A long lunch,' he commented.

'It's a lunch with the business community,' Fisher said smoothly. 'These things can go on.'

I bet, thought Georgiou.

Georgiou went back down to his office and dialled the superintendent's mobile number. When it answered, Georgiou could hear the droning chatter and clatter of glasses and bottles in the background that told him this lunch was everything he thought it would be.

'Stokes,' snapped the superintendent's voice.

'I'm sorry to disturb you, sir, but you did instruct me to tell you if there were any developments on the case—' began Georgiou.

'You mean you've got something?!' Stokes interrupted him, hopefully.

'Well, there have been developments which implicate someone . . .'

'The killer!' said Stokes excitedly. Then Georgiou heard him say smugly to whoever his companions were: 'My men think they've got a lead on him.' Then Stokes's voice was clear in Georgiou's ear again. 'Have you arrested him?'

'Not yet, sir . . .' began Georgiou.

'Why not?' demanded Stokes. 'We need a fast result on this!'

'First, he's vanished—'

'Vanished?!' echoed Stokes, angrily.

Before the Superintendent could say any more, Georgiou added, 'and he's one of our own team. Detective Richard Little.'

There was a silence that went on for so long that Georgiou might have thought they'd been cut off, if it wasn't for the background noise.

'Sir?' prompted Georgiou.

'You're to say nothing of this to anyone, Georgiou,' said Stokes, his voice suddenly low and conspiratorial. The background chatter on the phone had receded and Georgiou imagined that Stokes had moved away from his cronies to be out of earshot.

'But . . .' began Georgiou.

'Nothing,' snapped Stokes. 'Is that clear? Nothing. I shall

be at the office within the hour and I want to see you with everything you've got.'

Then the connection was cut.

Seward sat at the table in the canteen toying with the plate of vegetable chilli. Opposite her, Taggart stopped tucking into her steak and chips and looked at her partner, concerned.

'You OK?' she asked.

'Yeah, sure,' said Seward, forcing a smile. 'It's just this business of these murders. And Richard disappearing like that, and maybe the suspect.'

She hoped it sounded convincing. The truth was, last night was still hanging heavy over her. Georgiou being beaten up, seeing him with grazes and bruises, knowing he was in pain, made her want to pour her heart out to him about her feelings for him. Maybe that's what she should do. Maybe she should come right out with it to his face. Tell him she had feelings for him. That she loved him. No, that was too much at this stage. Just tell him she had feelings for him. Strong feelings. That she wanted to spend time with him. Personal time. That she wanted to take him in her arms and . . .

She must have let out a heartfelt sigh, because Taggart was looking at her, even more concerned than before.

'Are you *sure* you're all right?' asked Taggart.

'Yes. Absolutely,' insisted Seward.

'Only if there's anything you want to talk about. You know, nothing to do with the job . . .'

'No, I'm fine,' said Seward. Again, she forced a grin. 'It'll be OK once this particular job's over.'

*

Stokes paced around his office, shaking his head, an expression of horror on his face, as if his worst nightmare had arrived. Which, in a way, it had.

'How on earth can it be one of our men?' he demanded.

'We're not saying it is,' said Georgiou. 'All we're saying is that circumstantial evidence . . .'

'What about this terrorist?' demanded Stokes, and suddenly the superintendent was desperate for the murderer to be the terrorist he'd been so anxious to avoid. Anybody, rather than one of his own squad.

'There was no terrorist,' said Georgiou. 'GCHQ traced the website, and the video clip. It turned out to be some unhappy teenager in his bedroom in Cornwall, jumping on the bandwagon. No terrorist links at all, except in his head. He's currently under arrest. Or, at least, he was. I imagine he's been released back to his family while they work out what to charge him with.'

'It can't be one of ours! It can't be!' groaned Stokes. 'The press will have a field day! They'll wonder what sort of coppers we employ here! I'm going to come out of this looking like . . . like . . .'

Stokes stopped, lost for words. He shook his head numbly, shocked. 'This could finish me.'

'You can hardly be held responsible for the people you employ, sir,' said Georgiou. Though inside he thought: yes you can, and rightly so. It's about time some of the shit stuck to you. But then the other thought rose up again: if Richard Little was a rogue cop, Georgiou should have spotted it.

'What are we going to do?' asked Stokes, and this time he was really asking; almost begging Georgiou to come up with an answer that would save his skin. 'Isn't there some way we can keep this to ourselves?'

'No,' said Georgiou. 'If it is Richard Little who's the killer, and we don't know for sure it is – as I said, at the moment it's just circumstantial – then we have to warn the public against him. It would be even worse for us if we say nothing and he kills again.'

Stokes groaned, slumping down in his chair.

'There's got to be a way,' he appealed.

'One way would be to just say he's disappeared and put out an alert for him. We can say he's a member of the team investigating the killings and we think that stress has caused him to disappear. That way we can get his picture in the papers and on TV without anyone assuming he's the killer.'

'But we want the public to keep away from him, not run up to him if they see him and be sympathetic!'

'We add that because of his stress, Detective Little may be in a disturbed state, and members of the public are advised not to confront him but to get in touch with the police. It still doesn't give anything away. And if it turns out he's not the killer but just . . . run away . . . there's no harm done. No one knows.'

'Some smart alec journalist will put two and two together,' groaned Stokes.

'Not if we handle it properly,' said Georgiou. 'And not if we pick up Little quickly. And for that we need to use the media.'

TWENTY-EIGHT

The view from Castlerigg Stone Circle was breathtaking. Seward had been here a few times before, and each time it took her by surprise. No, surprise was the wrong word. Each time she was filled with a sense of awe. It wasn't just the stone circle itself, which – as stone circles went – was interesting enough, it was the setting: the fells of the North Lakes on all sides grim and imposing, and at the same time beautiful. No wonder the ancients had believed this place had magical properties. Even in this ultra-realistic non-believing twenty-first century, the power of the fells came through. This was nature at its most powerful, worthy of those ancient Britons erecting this circle of huge stones as a temple in its midst.

Right now the stone circle was buzzing with activity: cameras, cables, generators, all the trappings of a film company on location. In this case, scaled down to Eric Drake and his handful of student friends manhandling the equipment into place and shouting at one another to watch out for this and take care of that.

Seward and Taggart stood and watched the activity. At

the centre of it all was Eric Drake, and Seward couldn't deny that he was the hub of everything, stomping around, giving out orders, checking the camera, the equipment and the costumes. When they'd met him first in his room he had given the appearance of laziness to the level of sloth. The Eric Drake here was a different person altogether: high energy and organization.

'Shall we check them off against the list?' asked Taggart. She had a clipboard containing the names Drake had given them, the cast and crew.

'Yes, but I suggest we do it with the help of one of the people standing round doing nothing,' said Seward. 'Less confusion for us.'

Taggart nodded and they selected one of the young women who was also holding a clipboard with papers attached to it.

'Police,' said Seward, holding out her ID.

'Yes,' said the girl. 'Drake said you'd be here today. Exciting, isn't it?'

'Certainly busy,' said Taggart noncommittally.

She showed her clipboard with the list of names to the girl.

'We just need to check and see who's here and who isn't,' she said. 'As you know them, if you could point them out to us as I give you their names . . .'

'Of course,' said the girl.

One by one, as Taggart read out the names and ticked them off on her list, the girl pointed that person out. When they finished, Seward and Taggart did a quick count of the people milling around.

'There are about half a dozen here whose names aren't on

the list,' pointed out Taggart.

'Yes, well, when you make a film you always get a few more people turning up,' said the girl. 'Most of them are friends of people on the film.'

'Maybe we'd better go and find out who the others are,' suggested Taggart. 'Make sure we've got everybody's names.'

Seward nodded. To the girl, she said: 'It's important we have the names of *everyone* who's involved with this film. Are you sure this is everyone?'

'Oh yes,' said the girl, nodding. Then she thought for a moment, and added: 'Except for Jamie.'

'Who?' asked Taggart.

'Jamie,' she said. 'He's a helper.'

'What? A gofer? A runner? Whatever they call it?'

The girl shook her head. 'He's kind of a history nut. He helps Drake with the details. You know, getting them right.'

'So why isn't his name on the list of crew?'

'Well, he's not really crew. And I think he and Drake had a row over something.'

'Over what?'

'I think it was to do with the history or something.'

Seward felt a tingle up the back of her spine, like an invisible antennae had just picked up a vibration.

'What to do with the history?' she asked.

The girl shrugged. 'I don't know,' she said. 'It was just something between Drake and him. I don't really know about history. Film's my thing.'

'What's Jamie's full name?' pressed Seward.

Again, the girl shook her head.

'I don't know,' she said. 'He's just ... Jamie.' She

shrugged. 'Drake might know.'

But Seward was already hurrying to where Drake was standing in the middle of the stone circle, setting up a scene. A girl dressed in what looked like a flimsy nightdress was lying on the ground. A young man was kneeling next to her, checking her through a viewfinder.

'OK,' Drake was saying to the young man. 'This shot is from the crow's point of view, right . . .'

'Mr Drake,' said Seward. 'We need to talk to you.'

'Sure,' said Drake. 'After we've done this shot.'

'Now,' said Seward firmly.

By now Taggart had caught up with Seward, her notebook open and her pen poised.

'We're on a very tight schedule,' protested Drake. 'The light is vital . . .'

'So is our enquiry,' said Seward. 'What can you tell us about Jamie?'

Drake frowned. 'Who?' he asked.

'Jamie,' repeated Seward. 'Your history expert.'

Drake laughed, scornfully. 'Oh him! The nerd!'

'Yes,' said Seward. 'Why isn't he here today?'

Drake shrugged. 'We had an artistic disagreement,' he said. 'Not that there's any "art" in that idiot! He is so bloody pedantic! Wants everything to be "authentic", as he calls it. I told him, this film is art, not some boring documentary.'

'What's his full name?' pressed Seward.

Drake shrugged again. 'I don't know. Just . . . Jamie.'

'You work with him and you don't know his name?'

'I didn't work with him, as you call it. He just turned up one day when we were doing some shots up here and we got talking about history of the stones and stuff.'

'Where does he live?'

'I don't know,' he said. 'We didn't socialize. He wasn't my kind of person.' Then he added grudgingly, 'Well, he *was,* until he started getting all precious about *facts* and stuff.'

Seward looked around at the others, still busy preparing for shooting the film scene.

'Is there anyone here who had more to do with this Jamie than anyone else? Anyone he was friendly with?'

Drake shook his head. 'I don't think so,' he said. 'Like I say, he wasn't really our kind of person.'

'We're going to need to talk to everyone here, and we need to talk to them today,' said Seward.

'But the film . . .' began Drake, angrily.

'We won't interfere with your filming,' said Seward calmingly. 'You just go ahead. We'll talk to those people who are not involved at that time, or just hanging around. And then, when you break, we'll talk to your main crew.'

Drake nodded. 'OK,' he said. Curious, he asked: 'You think Jamie could be the one? The killer?'

'Who knows?' answered Seward noncommittally. 'At the moment we're just gathering facts.'

TWENTY-NINE

'What have you got?' asked Georgiou.

He'd been sitting at his desk, going through the reports again, looking for a common connection to the murders, when the door of the office had opened and Tennyson had entered with a mournful look on his face and dropped into a chair with a heartfelt sigh.

'It looks like Diane Moody's not our murderer,' groaned Tennyson.

Georgiou did his best to hide his smile. Frankly, he'd never thought she was, but he'd been wrong before, and Tennyson had appeared very convinced that Diane Moody was a prime suspect.

'Oh?' said Georgiou.

Tennyson nodded. 'I did some checking. Her alibis for the times the murders occurred hold firm. She was in bed with a lady vicar.'

Georgiou raised an eyebrow.

'It turns out they're an item. Have been for five years. Seems they're even thinking of making it official with one of these civil ceremonies.'

'And how did you find this out?'

'I asked Diane Moody where she was, and then checked it out with the lady vicar. She said they're like an old married couple. They go to bed at eleven o'clock every night, and don't get up till about seven the next morning.'

'No chance of Diane Moody sneaking out during the night?'

Tennyson shook his head. 'The vicar's a kind of semi-insomniac. Gets up a lot during the night. Moody, on the other hand, sleeps like a log, and – according to the vicar – snores like one being sawn up.'

'So, strike Moody.'

Tennyson nodded.

'Which leaves us with Richard Little,' murmured Georgiou. 'And a lot of very bad publicity.'

His phone rang.

'Georgiou,' he said.

It was Seward.

'We think we've got something,' she said. 'The strongest suspect yet.'

Georgiou felt his heart leap.

'Who?' he asked.

'That's the problem,' said Seward. 'So far we've only got a first name and a description. But we think he's looking good.'

'Where are you?' asked Georgiou.

'Castlerigg Stone Circle, Keswick,' replied Seward. 'Drake's here making his film. We've been talking to him and his pals.'

'How many of them are there?'

'About two dozen. Some are cast and crew, a few are just hangers-on. But we've picked up some info about a character called Jamie. He's not here, but he fits the profile. History nut. Fastidious to the point of obsession. He knew Tamara. I think he might be our killer.'

'Stay there,' said Georgiou. 'Tennyson and I will come over and join you. Four of us taking statements will speed things up. And we'll bring an e-fit artist with us and get the descriptions put into visual form and get it out to the media. With a bit of luck we may make the TV bulletins tonight.'

He hung up. Tennyson was looking at him quizzically.

'A suspect?' asked Tennyson.

'According to Seward,' replied Georgiou. 'Let's hope she's right.'

Seward was watching out for Georgiou and Tennyson and hurried towards them as they came through the field gate towards the stone circle.

'Tell me,' said Georgiou.

'Jamie,' said Seward. 'Age, mid to late twenties. Drives a dark-coloured van, but no one seems to remember the number. Local Carlisle accent. Very neat. The inside of his van was always tidy. His clothes were casual but always spotlessly clean. Someone said they thought even his jeans look liked he'd pressed them.'

'Fastidious,' murmured Georgiou, nodding.

'According to Drake, Jamie's obsessed with the Ancient Britons: the way they lived, their rituals, and especially the fact that the Romans conquered them and almost wiped them out. Again, according to Drake, Jamie was a bore about both the Ancient Britons and the Romans. He reckoned Jamie could go on *Mastermind* with them as his special subject and win it easily.'

'Better and better,' said Georgiou.

'The problem is, we don't know what his second name is, where he lives, where he works, *if* he works. All we know is what we picked up from Drake and his crowd, and they only ever met him when they were out and about doing stuff for Drake's film at places like Castlerigg and other ancient sites. It seems that Jamie knew where most of the ancient sites were.'

'It doesn't mean our killer *is* this Jamie,' pointed out Tennyson. 'It could still be Richard.'

'I know,' said Georgiou. 'But I'm hoping it isn't.'

He gestured towards the field gate.

'We've got an e-artist parked in his van out in the lane just outside the field. I want everyone here to talk to the artist so he can get their descriptions of this character. And do it one at a time so we get accurate memories. One may recall him having a mole on his cheek, or his hair being parted a certain way, or whatever, and if they start doing it as a group we could lose those identifying marks.'

'Will do,' said Seward.

Tennyson looked towards the stone circle, where the girl on the ground was being terrorized by an obviously fake bird made out of papier-mâché.

'How's the film?' he asked.

'It's crap,' said Seward. 'Worthy of Ed Wood at his worst.'

With that she went to join Taggart, who was talking to some of the crowd of students watching the filming.

Tennyson turned to Georgiou, puzzled.

'Who's Ed Wood?' he asked.

Georgiou shrugged. 'No one I know,' he said.

THIRTY

At six o'clock Georgiou was sitting in the office of Dan
Murphy at the offices of the *Cumberland News*. On
Murphy's desk was a mock-up of a front page of its daily
sister paper, the *News and Star*, for the next day, with the
e-fit artist's portrait impression of Jamie below a headline
which read 'Do You Know This Man?' Tennyson had taken
the e-fit to both BBC Television and Border TV to ensure
their coverage on that evening's news bulletins.

'Technology, eh,' said Murphy, grinning. 'Do you
remember the old days before all this digital stuff? A day
to put together a photo-fit, then another day of your lot
photocopying it and sending it out to the press, and then
another day before it would go into print. Now, contact's
done within minutes. Your artist guy e-mails me this, and
our reporter puts a piece together, all on the screen. Ten
minutes. Fantastic.'

Georgiou looked at the man in the picture. A young,
narrow face that seemed old and hard at the same time.
Short, dark hair, neatly trimmed. Clean shaven. Blue eyes.
The caption read 'The police would like to interview this

man to help eliminate him from their enquiries. If you think you know this man, please telephone . . .' and then followed the number, at which Georgiou had arranged for a large staff to handle the phone calls he hoped would flood in by way of response.

'You think it's him?' asked Murphy.

'I hope so,' said Georgiou. 'He's the strongest lead we've got.'

'What about your missing detective?' asked Murphy.

'That's a different issue,' said Georgiou. 'He's just gone missing and we need to find him for his own safety.'

Murphy chuckled.

'Yeah, and pigs might fly,' he said. 'That won't look good for you if it does turn out to be one of your own.'

Changing the subject, Georgiou asked: 'Is Jenny McAndrew in the office at the moment?'

'Your nemesis?' queried Murphy. 'Yes, she is, but I told her to stay out of the way while you were here, after what you'd said. Why?'

'I've got a story for her she may be interested in,' said Georgiou.

'What story?' asked Murphy.

'I'll tell you at the same time I tell her,' replied Georgiou.

'Why?'

'I want to see how surprised she is.'

Murphy shrugged, then left the office and returned a few minutes later with a young woman behind him. Jenny McAndrew looked every bit as Georgiou had imagined her: small, thin, nervous, her clothes fashionably expensive, but subdued in colour. She looked like what she wanted to be: a media person on the fast track to success.

'Jenny McAndrew, Inspector Georgiou,' said Murphy, making the introductions.

'Inspector,' said McAndrew warily.

'Ms McAndrew.' Georgiou nodded.

'The inspector says he's got a story for you,' said Murphy.

'Oh?' said McAndrew, guardedly.

'Of course, you may already know it,' said Georgiou. 'We arrested Ian Parks and three of his pals for grievous bodily harm yesterday.'

'Yesterday?' echoed Murphy. 'And you're only telling us today?'

'I thought with her contacts, Ms McAndrew might already know about it,' said Georgiou. He had been watching her the whole time, and could see that the news had genuinely come as a surprise to her.

'No,' she said. 'I didn't know.'

'I'm surprised, because it seems that the Parks family have a direct line to you,' said Georgiou. 'As does Councillor Maitland. But you say none of them have been in touch with you?'

McAndrew nodded. 'That's right,' she said, and Georgiou could feel the defensiveness rising up in her. She had been caught out in some way, but she didn't know how, or why, and it was making her angry.

'Perhaps because this time we have a confession, which makes it harder to deny the charge,' suggested Georgiou. 'We're also looking into racism as a possible motive for the offences.'

'Racism?' said Murphy.

Georgiou nodded.

'I thought, as Ms McAndrew wants to earn her spurs as an investigative journalist, it might be a story she might want to look into. It's the sort of theme that the big London papers love: racism mixed with violence.'

McAndrew studied Georgiou.

'Are you suggesting that there is some sort of collusion between the Parks family and Councillor Maitland, to do with racist politics?'

Georgiou shrugged. 'You're the investigative reporter,' he said. 'I'm just a detective. I'm sure you can do your own digging on any links that might exist between the people involved—'

'So you're saying—' cut in McAndrew, and now Georgiou could tell all her ambitions to be a top-line national reporter were kicking in in a big way.

'I'm saying nothing,' Georgiou interrupted her, 'except that four youths have been charged with grievous bodily harm. We believe there is a racist element to the attacks. And I'm surprised that you haven't been kept informed of this latest development by your usual contacts.'

With that Georgiou stood up and turned to Murphy.

'Thanks, Dan,' he said. 'If we get any feedback on anything, you'll be the first to know.'

'I'll walk you to the lift,' said Murphy.

As they left Murphy's office, out of the corner of his eye Georgiou saw McAndrew rush off. He guessed she was heading for her desk to start this new hot story.

'You're putting her on to Maitland,' said Murphy. 'You want him shown up for a racist. Get him kicked off the

Police Authority.'

Georgiou shrugged.

'I don't even know if he is a racist,' he said. 'But let's say that some digging into his politics won't do any harm. He is, after all, a servant of the public. The public have a right to know.'

'And if he's clean?' asked Murphy.

Georgiou smiled. 'A clean politician? Then I will be delighted to find that out.'

THIRTY-ONE

The evening broadcast on the television news brought in a wave of phone calls, and the picture of 'Jamie' in the *News and Star* the next morning added to it. By lunchtime Georgiou and his team had a list of callers who said they knew where Jamie lived, the make of van he drove, and from people he'd done work for. His name, they learnt, was James Oliver Willis. He was a general handyman in his late twenties who did all sorts of jobs, including electrical and plumbing work. But at the address they'd got for him in Carlisle's Brook Street at the back of Warwick Road, they drew a blank.

'He was here, but he left the day before yesterday,' said his former landlady, Mrs Irene Dodge. 'He was no trouble. Very polite. Very clean. Always cleared up after himself. Not like some tenants.'

'How long was he with you?' asked Georgiou.

'About six months,' said Mrs Dodge.

'How did he pay his rent?' asked Tennyson.

'Very regularly,' said Mrs Dodge. 'He was never late with it, not once.'

'I meant, *how* did he pay it? By cheque? Credit card? Was it paid by Social Services?'

'Oh no, nothing like that,' said Mrs Dodge. 'Cash every time.'

It was the same story with the people they talked to who James Willis had done work for. He would take cash only.

'He said he didn't have a bank account,' said one man, for whom Jamie had done some electrical work. 'Said he didn't believe in banks.'

Nor did he have a credit card. Nor a mobile phone. However, he did have his van registered with the DVLA, and taxed, and fully MOT'd, all done just five months before, one month after he'd moved into Mrs Dodge's house.

'Where was he before that?' asked Georgiou as he and Tennyson drove back to the office. 'There are no records of him even existing before he turned up at Mrs Dodge's. Nothing.'

'Maybe he set up a fake new identity when he moved in with her?' suggested Tennyson.

'It's possible,' agreed Georgiou. 'In which case, any info we get back from DVLA at Swansea, his so-called date of birth, et cetera, isn't going to be a lot of use.'

'We've still got to go through it, though, guv,' Tennyson pointed out.

By the time they got back to the office the amount of information coming in about James Willis was turning into an avalanche. Phone messages from people who'd met him in a pub: 'He was on our table in the pub quiz. He knew so much about history! We almost won the quiz that night!' All of them said the same: a very neat and nice young man.

Very polite. A perfect worker, always left the place neat and tidy after he'd done a job. Some commented that they'd seen him out running through the local parks. 'He kept himself very fit. He was always exercising. And he was strong! He lifted my boiler out all on his own!'

'So where is he now?' asked Georgiou. 'He can't have just suddenly disappeared into thin air!'

'Gone just like he was before,' commented Seward. 'He appeared out of thin air. He's vanished back there.'

Georgiou's mobile rang. He checked the number. It was Conway.

'Georgiou,' he said.

'We've got him, boss,' Conway told him.

'Jamie?' asked Georgiou.

'What?' came Conway's voice. 'No. Richard. He's turned up in Manchester. I'm taking a couple of uniformed with me to collect him now and bring him in, just in case.'

THIRTY-TWO

R ichard Little sat in the same chair in the same interview room where Ian Parks had sat earlier. He looked
a mess. His clothes looked like he'd been sleeping in them.
His pale face wasn't just unshaven, it was grimy. He stank
of dirt, sweat and alcohol, a mixture of vodka and gin,
Georgiou guessed. His eyes were red-rimmed. The fastidious
Richard Little of just a few days ago had gone, to be replaced
with a dishevelled tramp.

'I'm sorry,' he said. He sat with his shoulders slumped, a
man beaten down by everything. 'I didn't know what else to
do. I couldn't face it. I couldn't cope with it.'

'With what?' asked Georgiou gently.

Georgiou sat on the other side of the table to Little, with
Conway sitting next to him. A uniformed officer stood by the
door.

Little sighed, shook his head, then said: 'Vera's got a
lover.'

A lover? Georgiou looked at Conway to see if this was
something he knew about, but Conway gave a brief shake of
his head. This was news to him.

'It's our next-door neighbour,' he said. 'Vincent Driscoll,' he added, almost spitting out the name with venom. 'Driscoll's wife died about two years ago. Last Christmas we thought it would be a nice thing for him to come and join us for Christmas dinner. He hasn't got any family of his own and we guessed he'd be lonely.'

'Whose idea was that?' asked Georgiou. 'Yours or Vera's?'

'Vera's,' said Little. 'Personally, I like to spend Christmas my own way, but Vera said it was the right thing to do. So he came and had Christmas dinner with us. And afterwards he started popping in for a chat and a bit of company, as he put it.'

Richard fell silent, and Georgiou could see that he was running over all that had happened since that Christmas in his mind.

'What makes you think she was having an affair?' he asked.

'About two months ago I caught them in the kitchen, kissing. As I came in they moved apart and just carried on as if everything was normal, as if there was nothing going on. I think they didn't think I'd spotted them, because they'd moved apart too quick, but I could tell. After that they were more careful, but I could tell something was going on between them. So one night I told Vera I was going to be on night duty for a special operation down in the south of the county.'

'The south?' queried Georgiou. 'Surely she realized that we don't operate there.'

'Like I say, I told her it was a special operation. A joint forces operation. I told her I wouldn't be back until six the following morning.'

'And instead you hid and watched your house,' said Georgiou.

Little nodded.

'Sure enough, at midnight, Driscoll came out of his house and went into mine. I stayed watching all night. He came out at four o'clock and went back to his own house.'

'Why didn't you confront him?' asked Conway.

'Because I didn't know what to do!' burst out Little. 'I love Vera. If she knew I'd spent the night spying on them, and that I'd lied to her about being on special operation, what would she think of me? What would she say to me?'

'She'd lied to you,' Georgiou pointed out.

'I know,' said Little. 'But it didn't make what I'd done any better. It would have showed her that I didn't trust her.'

'And you were right not to,' said Conway. 'Richard, she was cheating on you.'

Little dropped his head.

'I know,' he said.

Then he looked up at both men, tears running down his grimy face, his face a desperate appeal to them.

'I've always done the right thing,' he said. 'Always. My whole life. It isn't fair! Life isn't fair!'

THIRTY-THREE

Seward pulled into the parking area at the back of the small block of flats where she lived in Rickergate. It was a small discreet development tucked away from the main road, close to the town centre, and with resident parking. The parking space alone was worth its weight in gold. As Carlisle had expanded in recent years, so had the number of cars, and No Parking signs were now everywhere. Seward often thought it would be a good idea to sell her car and rent out her parking space to motorists desperate to find somewhere to put their vehicles. It was a potential gold-mine. Of course, there would be the downside of having to travel everywhere by taxi.

As she walked towards the entrance of the flats she thought about the search for James Willis. It had been just twenty-four hours since his e-fit likeness had appeared in newspapers and on television screens across the whole country, and yet no one had reported seeing him. Where was he? How could anyone hide out like that in this technological day and age? She felt a sting in her neck, and her hand flew up to swat away whatever insect it was. She felt a numbness spreading out from where she'd been stung and her thought was, It must be some big wasp ... And then, as the numbness spread and her vision began to go, she realized it was something more.

Georgiou sat at home watching a television programme about cooking. Georgiou wasn't particularly interested in cooking, but he'd flicked through the other channels and found they were either programmes filled with alleged celebrities who he'd never heard of doing stupid things, or programmes about haunted houses, or dramas which were either about hospitals or the police. He'd even found one in which a police inspector was also a doctor, so he guessed the television company were hedging their bets. He was surprised they hadn't thought about making the medical police inspector a celebrity chef to cover all bases.

He thought about turning the television off and listening to the radio, or to some music, but he knew his mind would just turn back to the case, and he felt like he needed a break from it. The killer was James Willis, Georgiou was sure of it. Now all they had to do was find him.

Where was he? How could anyone disappear so completely and so easily in this day and age? The country was supposed to be swamped with closed circuit television cameras and surveillance equipment. Every move anyone made could, in theory, be tracked within seconds by spy satellites and computer checks. But Willis had been careful about that. No credit card to be picked up. No mobile phone to be traced.

Where was he staying? Georgiou guessed he was hiding out somewhere in the country. The reports had said that he used to go for long runs in the country to keep fit. There were still large empty places in the north of England, and across the border in Scotland. Places where someone could go to ground and hide. Cumbria was the second emptiest county in England, and North Yorkshire the first. Southern Scotland was filled with enormous forests, and further north was the vast areas of the Highlands. All were within easy reach by van from Carlisle.

Why hadn't the van been spotted yet? Easy. Because he reckoned Willis had changed the number plates and then altered the van in some way. Stuck a transfer on its plain side, a logo giving the name of a company. Painted a white stripe down a side. Simple disguise.

His thoughts turned to Richard Little and the small detective's impassioned look at Georgiou as he'd blurted out: 'Life isn't fair!'

No, thought Georgiou, life isn't. Dictators murder millions and steal a country's wealth, and live to a ripe old age in luxury in a country that is prepared to keep them safe and secure. Murders and rapists and muggers go free, while a retired vicar gets sent to a high-security prison because he can't afford to pay the increase in his council tax. Young kids are sent to war and die in their hundreds, ill equipped and without the proper weapons and ammunition to defend themselves, while other people get rich off the profits of that same war. Some vile people do unspeakable things and live to a ripe old age, while others – good people – die young. Like Susannah. No, life isn't fair. But it's all we have.

The sound of his phone ringing brought him out of his reverie.

'Georgiou,' he said.

It was Jenny McAndrew.

'Inspector,' she said, in the same over-familiar cheery tones she'd used on her first phone call. 'I have some news you may be interested in.'

'On James Willis?' he hazarded.

'On your old friend, Councillor Maitland,' said McAndrew. 'I did a bit of digging into his political past. I thought you'd like to know there'll be a story in tomorrow's *News and Star*. I'll read it to you.' Before Georgiou could interrupt, McAndrew had launched into reading her report: 'Councillor Quits In Racism Row. Councillor John Maitland has resigned from the Police Authority after allegations over his associations with a far right political organization. Investigations by this newspaper uncovered the fact that Councillor Maitland was a member of the National Front when he lived in Oldham in Lancashire in the 1980s, and that he had also signed petitions supporting the forced repatriation of foreign nationals from the United Kingdom, as well as the forced repatriation of British-born people of foreign descent.'

'You got him on a signature on a couple of petitions!' said Georgiou incredulously. 'How on earth did you do that? You can't have had time to go through a couple of pretty ancient petitions name by name!'

'Well, between you and me, Inspector, I may have – shall we say – projected that fact from information received.'

'You made it up,' said Georgiou.

'No,' said McAndrew. 'I had good information from someone who knew him in Oldham that Maitland actually organized these petitions in his part of Oldham, so it's fairly safe to guess that he must have signed them. Of course, if he disputes it, we can dig out the petitions and present them as evidence to back up my report, and I'm fairly sure we'll find his signature on them. But right now I don't think he'll be wanting to stir anything like that up, do you?'

'But he resigned?'

'Not without protest,' said McAndrew. 'But Ted Armstrong, the chairman of the Police Authority, insisted. And the other members of the Police Authority backed him up so fast it was almost embarrassing. None of them want to be seen as supporting a former racist. Clean hands are needed for politics, eh?'

'He used you,' said Georgiou. 'Maitland. And the Parks family. To get at me.'

'And now you've used me to get rid of Maitland,' said McAndrew. 'And, to be frank, it doesn't bother me. I don't mind being used if I get something out of it. I see it as a fair exchange. Anyway, I thought you'd like to know.'

'Thank you,' said Georgiou. 'And . . . thank you for your investigation into Maitland. With talent like that, you ought to join the police.'

McAndrew chuckled.

'No thank you, Inspector. I like to play on all sides of the fence. But make sure you get a copy of tomorrow's paper. We need the sales.'

'I will. And thanks.'

As Georgiou hung up, he couldn't resist a little smile of satisfaction. Maitland gone. But he'd be back, in some other form. People like that couldn't stay away.

There was the sound of his doorbell buzzing. He looked at the clock. Half past ten. A bit late for someone to be calling.

There was no one outside when he opened his front door. Someone playing stupid tricks, he thought. Then he saw the piece of paper on the ground, held there by a small pebble. He bent down to pick it up, and there was a sudden pain at the back of his head, and everything went black.

THIRTY-FOUR

When Georgiou came to, his first thought was that his head was going to explode. Pain seared across the back of his skull. His second thought was the realization that he was on a wooden chair with his hands and legs securely tied. Very securely.

He was tied to one of his own chairs in his own kitchen. Sitting at his kitchen table watching him, his face impassive, was the face that had been in all the newspapers and on all the television screens. James Willis. Jamie.

'Hurts, doesn't it?' said Willis.

Georgiou said nothing. His mind was racing, wondering how he could get out of this. Tentatively he pulled at ropes that held him.

'You won't break them,' said Willis. 'Electrical wire. Remember. Like the others. Very strong.'

'You're going to kill me?' said Georgiou.

Willis shook his head. 'No,' he said. 'You're going to commit suicide.'

Georgiou laughed sarcastically. 'In your dreams!' he said.

'At least, that's what it's going to look like,' continued

Willis. He produced a sheet of paper and held it out so that Georgiou could see the words on it. 'I used your computer to write your suicide note. It's all there. How it was you who killed them. How you fixed everything to try and make it look like someone else, but then guilt overcame you.'

'Oh?' said Georgiou.

Willis seemed very comfortable, very relaxed. Very neat as well. His clothes were clean. His hair was washed. His face was neatly shaved. He didn't give the appearance of a man who'd been living rough for the past few days. Once again, Georgiou gave a tug at the wires that tied him to the chair, but it was just as Willis said, they were very tight, very secure. There was no way he was going to get out of them.

Keep Willis talking, Georgiou thought. The longer he talks, the more chance you've got of getting out of this. 'Why would I want to kill those people? I didn't know them.'

'Grief,' said Willis. 'Revenge against the world. Your wife died and it sent you over the edge. Then, when you were suspended, it made you angry at the police.' Seeing Georgiou's surprise, Willis smiled and added: 'You see, Inspector, I've been following your career. Only when you've been in the papers, of course. I'm not a stalker. But fortunately very little happens in this part of Cumbria, so a Greek detective is news.'

'I'm not Greek,' said Georgiou.

'Especially one who gets suspended,' continued Willis, ignoring Georgiou's denial.

'You won't get away with this,' said Georgiou. 'You've left too many clues.'

Willis laughed out loud, a sound that sent a chill through Georgiou.

'Oh, I love that phrase,' he said, mimicking '"You won't get away with it!" Yes I will, Inspector. And I will just disappear. And then I'll reinvent myself. Just like I did when I came here six months ago.'

'Who are you?' asked Georgiou. 'Where are you from, exactly?'

Willis shook his head.

'Oh no, Inspector. We haven't got time for that. And anyway, that's all in the past, and the so-called experts tell you that it's not what happened in the past that matters, but what happens in the future.'

The so-called experts, thought Georgiou. Counsellors. Psychiatrists. He's been locked up, having treatment.

'But we know that's not true, don't we, Inspector?' Willis carried on. 'We know it's the past that makes us what we are. Where we've come from. What we've done. What's happened to us.'

'At the risk of using another cliché,' said Georgiou as calmly as he could, 'they won't believe it was me.'

'Yes, they will,' said Willis, 'especially when they find the new body here at Bowness. One of your own.'

One of my own? thought Georgiou.

Willis obviously saw the look of alarm on Georgiou's face, because he smiled.

'Yes,' he said, nodding. 'She's in the back of my van at the moment, nicely tied up and sleeping like a baby.'

From his pocket he produced an air pistol.

'Tranquilizer dart in the neck,' he said. 'She never knew

what hit her. She'll be out for . . . ooh . . . ages. She might not even wake up before I do what I have to do.'

'And what's that?' asked Georgiou.

Again, Willis laughed.

'Really, Inspector, don't pretend to be naïve. I am going to hang her up and cut her head off, of course, just like the others.'

'Who is it?' asked Georgiou. Although he was trying to present a calm front to Willis, he could feel his heart pounding, feel an icy sweat.

'One of your detective sergeants,' said Willis. 'The butch one with the short hair. DS Seward, I think.'

Georgiou shook his head.

'You're lying,' he said.

'Really?' said Willis with a smile.

He took a small black folder from his pocket, opened it, and tossed it on the table for Georgiou to see. It was Seward's warrant card.

'So?' said Georgiou. 'You could have got that any way. Picked her pocket.'

Willis smiled again and shook his head.

'Really, Inspector,' he said. 'Why on earth should I lie about this? You're going to die very shortly. I thought it would be interesting for you to know this last part of my plan.'

'Why should I be interested?' asked Georgiou.

'Because you need to know that in the end we beat you.'

Georgiou frowned.

'Beat me?' he echoed. 'Who?'

'Not you, Inspector. Your race. The Romans and Greeks.

The so-called conquerors of the world.'

'I'm not Greek!' exploded Georgiou angrily. 'I'm British!'

Willis shook his head.

'No, you're not,' he said. 'The British were almost wiped out by your kind two thousand years ago. But we survived. Some of us. We never went away. You tried to wipe us out but we came back.'

Now the smile and any hint of humour, ironic or otherwise, had gone from Willis. As he looked at Georgiou, his eyes burnt with passion and hatred and anger, like one of the revivalist preachers Georgiou had seen on the screen in old films. Or like some of the radical Imams who preached Islamic purity, rousing their followers up to kill all unbelievers.

'You came here to conquer us, the greatest military machine the world had ever known. The Roman army had conquered the whole of the known world, and now it tried to conquer Britain. But it couldn't, because it had never faced an enemy like the British. Pure fighting spirit. A warrior race like no other.'

'The Romans fought plenty of other so-called warrior nations,' said Georgiou, racking his memory, searching for information from those history lessons at school. The names of the old tribes came to him: 'The Gauls in France. The German tribes.'

'Yes, but none of them so powerful that you needed to build a wall to control them.'

'The Romans were nothing to do with me,' repeated Georgiou firmly.

'The Roman Empire was built on the conquests of the

Greeks,' countered Willis. 'The Romans built their culture on what they took from the Greeks, so, to all intents and purposes, it was the Greco-Roman Empire. You are a Greek.'

'My father was from Cyprus. My mother was English. I was born in this country. I'm British.'

Willis shook his head.

'It's in the blood,' he said. 'Who we are, what we are. You're a Greek. The great conquerors. You and the Romans.'

He's mad, thought Georgiou. Absolutely mad. But terrifyingly clever with it.

'Your Roman allies built the wall. Seventy-four miles long, from coast to coast. It was said to be the greatest engineering achievement ever. But for the Britons it was a massive symbol of the greatest possible oppression.'

The wall, thought Georgiou. Diane Moody had been right. This had been about Hadrian's Wall.

'Haltwhistle, Birdoswald and Stanwix,' he murmured. 'Points along the wall.'

'Not just points,' said Willis. 'Major Roman forts. And Stanwix was the largest fort on the wall by far. And the second largest fort on the wall–'

'Was here,' Georgiou finished for him. 'At Bowness on Solway.'

Willis nodded. 'Maia, to give it its proper name,' he said. 'And what have you people here done? You have built a Roman temple here in this village to celebrate it!'

Georgiou shook his head. 'If you're referring to the building on The Banks, it's not a Roman temple,' he said.

The Banks, as the one open area of public amenity in the village was known, had been a place for the Edwardians

to sit on the grass and picnic and look out over the Solway
Firth in the early years of the twentieth century. As the
twentieth century had moved on, so time had taken its toll
on The Banks. Gravity had meant the paths had slipped. At
one point the local council had even talked about closing it
off as dangerous. Then the local village community group
had stepped in. They leased The Banks from the parish
council at a peppercorn rent and set about working with
local organizations to raise the money to restore it. This had
coincided with the opening of Hadrian's Wall Trail as a major
tourist walk. At the eastern end of the trail was Segedunum,
Wallsend in Newcastle. The other end of the trail, the official
western end of the wall, was at Bowness on Solway. And so
funding had been found to restore The Banks to its former
glory. And, as much of the money came through the official
tourist channels, it had been agreed that the renovation and
restoration should have a Roman theme. Plants that the
Romans had brought with them to Britain were planted.
Replica Roman pottery was made as decoration. A Roman-
style mosaic was created by the children from the village
school under the direction of a local artist. And the old brick
shelter with a corrugated tin roof had been demolished and
replaced with a new building from which keen birdwatchers
could shelter from the elements as they followed their hobby,
watching the wading birds and the geese out on the mudflats
of the Solway. To reinforce the Roman theme, this building
had been designed and constructed completely along Roman
lines. No nails had been used in its construction, just
wooden pegs, as the Romans had done. The roof had been
tiled with specially made replica Roman tiles. The building

was a marvel of Roman workmanship, 2000 years after the original craftsmen had worked at this same spot.

'It's a temple,' insisted Willis. 'And, as such, it's the perfect place for my last sacrifice. It even has stout wooden beams for me to hang your sergeant from.'

'There's no need to do this,' said Georgiou. 'Kill me, OK, if it satisfies some twisted sort of logic in your mind. But why kill my sergeant? You've made your point already with the other three bodies. You don't need another one.'

'It's the end of the wall, Inspector,' said Willis calmly. 'It will drive my message home, so there will be no mistake. Another headless body. The British way of war. It's a spit in the face of the Romans!'

'The Romans have gone!' insisted Georgiou desperately. 'They went sixteen hundred years ago. Not gloriously, either. They just faded away. Your precious Barbarians beat them.'

'But no one remembers that,' said Willis. 'There's nothing to mark them going. Just fading away, as you say. Well, people will remember now. Four headless bodies along the wall. And once they realize the message, they'll be waiting like scared rabbits for the next one. Where along the wall will it happen next? Wallsend? Corbridge? Chesters? Vindolanda? Housesteads? They'll be talking about this for years. Decades. Waiting for the next one. Terrified!'

'But why my sergeant?' repeated Georgiou.

'Because it makes it personal,' said Willis. 'It points the finger at you. She's murdered here by you. You commit suicide.' He smiled. 'I saw the two of you the other night here, coming out of the pub. Everyone will assume there was something between you that set you off.'

'And how am I supposed to commit suicide?'

'Whisky and sleeping pills,' said Willis. 'It's nice and uncomplicated. No messing about with guns and stuff, where they can use scientific tests to see which hand you used to fire it, that sort of thing.'

Willis produced a bottle of pills from his pocket.

'I bought the pills. A very common sort. Available in every chemist. And you have whisky here already, I see.'

For the first time Georgiou noticed his bottle of whisky on the table.

'I force them down your throat, and then it's off to your fake Roman temple with your unconscious sergeant. And that's it. All over.'

'Someone will see you,' said Georgiou. 'This is a very small village.'

'If they do, that'll be even better,' said Willis. 'I'll be wearing one of your coats and a hat pulled well down. But, to be honest, I doubt if anyone will be at The Banks at this time of night.'

Willis flipped the top off the bottle of pills.

'Well, I think we've talked enough, Inspector,' he said. 'It's been nice talking to you, but I have work to do.'

Georgiou watched Willis unscrew the top of the bottle of whisky and pour a large measure into a glass. There had to be a way out of this! There had to! He would jam his mouth shut and resist! But he knew he wouldn't be able to, not for long. Willis would clamp his nostrils shut tight, and sooner or later Georgiou would be forced to open his mouth, and then the whisky and the pills would be forced in. It wouldn't matter if the whisky spilled: the investigators would just assume that Georgiou was so drunk or drugged he couldn't control the glass.

Willis smiled and walked towards Georgiou, the whisky bottle in one hand, the bottle of pills in the other.

'Open wide,' he chuckled. 'Take your medicine like a good boy.'

Georgiou clamped his jaws shut tight and glared at Willis, who shook his head.

'Dear oh dear,' he said. 'It looks as if I'm going to have to be very strict with you.'

He put the bottle and pills down on the table, and then suddenly whirled round and smashed his fist into Georgiou's nose. Georgiou rocked backwards at the force of the blow and the chair tipped over, Georgiou crashing to the floor. The pain on his bound arms was excruciating, as was the pain in the centre of his face. He was sure his nose was broken. He could feel blood trickling down his throat.

Willis picked up the whisky bottle again, leaving one hand free.

'That's better,' he said, moving to stand over Georgiou. 'Now gravity can be our helper.'

And he reached down with his free hand and dug his fingers into the sides of Georgiou's mouth, prising his teeth apart, while at the same time upending the whisky bottle over Georgiou's blood-filled mouth. Georgiou resisted, trying to block the whisky with his tongue, but it was no good, Willis was too strong, his powerful grip slowly forcing Georgiou's mouth open wider . . .

The sound of glass shattering suddenly filled the kitchen, and the pressure on Georgiou's face was released as Willis fell back . . . and kept falling.

Then there was an even bigger sound of glass shattering, and Georgiou was suddenly aware that his window had been smashed in, and the barrel of a rifle was poking through the tatters of glass hanging from the frame.

Willis lay on the floor next to Georgiou, his face creased in pain, blood spreading out from a wound in his shoulder.

Then the kitchen was full of people. Men in black wearing body armour and armed with automatic rifles. And Debby Seward. She was the first to get to him, while the armed men were forcing the wounded Willis to lie face down with his hands and legs spread-eagled.

'It's OK!' said Seward.

She had half lifted Georgiou and was cutting at the electrical wire that tied his wrists with a pair of wire cutters.

'He said you were in the van,' said Georgiou. 'Unconscious.'

'Lucky for me I've got a strong constitution,' said Seward grimly. 'I came round quicker than our friend here allowed for. The trouble was he had me tied up like the others, so I couldn't get free.'

'Then how. . .?' asked Georgiou.

'I managed to get my hands on my mobile phone and texted Mac Tennyson. He arranged for the Armed Response Unit. While one lot were getting me out of the van, the rest were staking out your house, getting ready to bust in. When they saw Willis hit you they realized they had to act quickly.'

'I'm glad they did otherwise it would have been a stomach

pump job.'

Seward had finished cutting the wires that bound him, and Georgiou struggled to his feet. His head still ached. First the blow on the back of the head, then the hard punch in the face. And on top of being knocked unconscious just a few days before. His head was taking a lot of punishment lately.

He became aware of Tennyson joining them, his face a picture of worry.

'You OK, guv?' he asked.

'As well as can be expected, considering the circumstances,' said Georgiou.

Willis had been hauled to his feet and handcuffed.

'Watch that wound,' said Georgiou. 'We want him alive for trial.'

'Unfortunately,' said Tennyson sourly. 'OK, lads, get him in the ambulance.'

'An ambulance as well,' commented Georgiou.

'We guessed there might be a casualty,' said Tennyson. 'I'm just glad it's not you.' Then he looked closer at Georgiou, at the blood around his nose and mouth.

'Shall I get one of the paramedics to look at that?'

Georgiou shook his head.

'Cotton wool, a couple of aspirin, and a night's rest should do the trick,' he said.

'But doesn't it hurt?'

'Yes. If you must know, it hurts like hell. And I'm sure it'll still hurt tomorrow. But what will make it feel better is knowing we've got chummy safe and sound under lock and key.'

Tennyson nodded, and gestured towards Willis, who was being hustled out of the room. 'I'll just go and do the formal stuff, read him his rights, and I'll be back in a minute.'

Then Tennyson was gone.

'We'll put some plastic over the window, sir,' said one of the ARU. 'It'll keep out the draught tonight.'

'That's fine. Thanks,' said Georgiou.

He still felt groggy. He sat down and felt his nose. It seemed to be swelling up. Aspirin, cotton wool and rest; that's what he'd told Tennyson he needed. The truth was he just wanted shot of them all so he could collapse and suffer in the privacy of his own home.

Seward sat down near him and looked at him anxiously. She gulped, and then said:

'Look, I'm not sure you should be on your own tonight. Not after what's happened.'

'I'll be OK,' said Georgiou. 'You're the one who needs looking after.'

'I wasn't hit over the head. *Again.*'

'You still don't know if the tranquilizer has a knock-on effect,' pointed out Georgiou. 'If you ask me, you're the one who needs treatment.'

'Maybe I just need some rest,' she said. 'After all, we've caught the killer. Case closed.'

'Yes,' said Georgiou.

There was a pause between them. A difficult one. Both could feel it. Georgiou looked at Seward, at the expression on her face, the concern for him writ large, and he wanted to hold her, take her in his arms and say, 'Don't worry. I'll be fine.' But he knew that if he did it wouldn't stop there.

Not for him. Not tonight, not after all that had happened. Thinking that she was going to be savagely killed by Willis. Thinking of her as he sat tied to that chair, desperate to save her, but unable to move.

He looked at her, her eyes scanning his face, her hands clenching and unclenching with some sort of inner tension. Say it is just sympathy, like before, he thought, and I say something . . . make the wrong move. She's my sergeant, for God's sake! And a really good one. She would be in her rights to demand a transfer. And what would that do to me? To the squad?

Seward was the first one to break the difficult silence between them.

'Look,' she said, and even as she spoke she knew she sounded awkward and clumsy, but she had to say it. 'The way you are, the way I am . . .'

Before she could continue, Tennyson had returned and joined them.

'All done and dusted,' he said. 'He's been formally charged and the ARU are taking him to the infirmary to get the wound seen to. I've told them to keep an armed guard on him at all times.'

'Good,' said Georgiou.

Tennyson looked around the room.

'You'll need to get that window fixed,' he said, indicating the remains of the glass.

'I'll sort it out tomorrow,' said Georgiou.

'Right.' Tennyson nodded. Then he turned to Seward and said: 'I suppose you'll be wanting a lift back to Carlisle?'

Seward hesitated, shot a look at Georgiou, her eyes

making a silent appeal. But either Georgiou didn't see it, or he ignored it, because, after what Seward thought was the briefest of hesitations, he nodded and said: 'She will indeed, Mac. Thanks.'

Seward hesitated again, then nodded. But this time her eyes weren't on Georgiou. The fire had gone out of them. She stood up.

'Get some rest,' she said.

'And you,' he said. 'And if you don't feel OK in the morning—'

She cut him off with a shake of her head.

'I'll be in tomorrow,' she said. 'Don't worry about me.'

Then she walked out.

'See you tomorrow, guv,' said Tennyson. He grinned. 'A big score to us, eh!'

'Yes,' echoed Georgiou. 'A big score to us.'